All That Love Stuff

Patsy Collins

To Nikki Snelling, who has been my friend for so long I suspect she's forgotten that she's the bad influence and I'm the sensible one.

Contents

1. Written In The Stars

Because her parents moved home just after the start of term, Heidi had started junior school two days later than everyone else. As a consequence it seemed to her everyone else had friends and knew where to go and what to do, whilst she was lonely and lost.

The teachers did their best to help her settle. Their kindest action, from Heidi's point of view, was to agree when Carl begged to be allowed to show her around the school. He was months older, inches taller, clever and kind. Heidi loved him from then on.

They sat side by side in lessons, and in break times lay on their backs in the playground and looked for shapes in the clouds. Heidi often had tea at Carl's house. He came round to hers to watch cartoons. They went to the library together. He borrowed science books; she chose those with pictures of horses or kittens.

At school Heidi liked colouring and cooking. Carl asked their teachers questions, such as why clouds could go in different directions at the same time and if you could tell which country the rain had come from. It seemed he wanted to know everything.

The teachers hadn't always known. That was a shock to Heidi. Didn't grown-ups know everything and have all the answers? She'd said as much to Carl.

"Perhaps you just need to ask the right grown up," he'd told her.

He'd come back in the next day and explained to the class

about air currents and thermals.

It was the teacher's turn to ask a question. "How do you know all this, Carl?"

"I asked my dad's friend, Professor Edwards." The teacher knew who the professor was and agreed he was an excellent person to ask.

A few weeks later the professor came into class to talk to them all. His skin was dark and, as he strode to the front of the class, the large coat he'd draped over his shoulders billowed like a cape. Someone said he looked like a bat.

Professor Edwards must have heard as he said, "I act like one too, usually only coming out at night."

That got the kids' attention and he held it with amazing stories about the stars and beautiful pictures of the night sky. Heidi saw why Carl was so interested.

"He has his head in the clouds," her mum used to say. It was true in a way; Carl was fascinated by anything to do with the sky, clouds included.

As Carl and Heidi became older they got teased by other kids. Sometimes, because of their friendship, it was assumed they were boyfriend and girlfriend. Heidi blushed when it was suggested.

Carl said, "Who cares what they think?" When he was called a geek, he agreed that he was.

Heidi found such remarks harder to shrug off and a few thoughtless comments made her deeply self-conscious of her red hair and multitude of freckles. "I hate looking like this," she told him.

"But why?" Carl asked. "When the sun lights up your hair it's as brilliant as a solar flare and your freckles are like stars." He'd tried to find constellations on her face and skinny arms and legs.

Carl told her the answers for a lot of things were in the sky; the weather, how the world began, satellites.

"Like horoscopes?" Heidi asked.

"No, that's not the same thing at all... but I do think I'll find the answers to what my life will be in the stars."

Carl's sixteenth birthday party was held at an observatory. The guests went for a tour and looked through a huge telescope. Naturally Heidi was invited. She'd known she would be. She wasn't at all surprised to see Professor Edwards was there too. She was quite surprised to meet his daughter and find that she was about Heidi's age and very pretty. Carl had mentioned spending time with the Professor's family and that his daughter's name was Stella. Heidi hadn't taken a great deal of notice, except to consider the name appropriate and imagine calling her and Carl's children after astronomical features. Andromeda perhaps or Jupiter; wasn't that the planet he'd said had days longer than the years? She should have paid more attention.

Stella was tall and slender with skin as dark and velvety perfect as the night sky. Her laughing eyes sparkled like unexplored galaxies and her ready smile glowed like the crescent moon. All that was bad enough, but the worst thing was that Carl obviously liked her and the two of them chatted easily. Until then Heidi thought she was the only girl Carl ever spoke to. At school he was shy around anyone female, especially those who showed any interest in him. Plenty did.

Heidi was concerned. Maybe Carl, clever though he was, hadn't seen what was obvious to her; that they were destined to be together always. She was running out of opportunities to show him. Carl went on to sixth form at the same school as Stella attended. Heidi got a job in a veterinary surgery and went to college one day a week.

They remained friends, meeting up after school and at weekends, sometimes just the two of them but more often in a group. Annoyingly the group often included Stella. Thankfully Carl showed no signs of wanting Stella to be his girlfriend, but then he didn't show signs of wanting anyone else to be his girlfriend, Heidi included. He no longer seemed nervous of girls, but kept his distance from any who made it clear friendship wasn't exactly what they had in mind. Heidi was careful not to push him away like that or to show her jealousy of Stella who was obviously important to him. She continued that behaviour when Carl, and Stella, went to university.

Heidi met up with Carl occasionally. They exchanged a few letters and a lot of emails. Still he showed no sign that his feelings for her in any way matched what she felt for him.

"He's young, concentrating on his career and carried away with his success. Give him time to come back down to earth," her mum said.

She'd been right. Carl had written well respected papers on astronomy and even been on television several times. The first time was almost accidental. A documentary was made about the latest astronomical research methods and the presenter interviewed several students. Carl got such a good response for the clarity and humour in his explanations that he'd been invited onto other shows, particularly those for children. That, combined with his study, left him little time for anything else.

Even before his degree was confirmed officially, Carl was offered the job he wanted, studying his beloved stars and doing outreach work at the observatory.

"That's brilliant news, Carl," Heidi said hugging him.

"Fantastic isn't it? Especially as it's closer to home. I'll be able to see more of you and work with Professor Edwards, and Stella of course."

"Yeah, lovely."

"What do you mean?"

Ooops, she'd almost let her jealousy show. Better say something nice. "It seems right that you'll work with Professor Edwards. It was him who really got you interested in astronomy, wasn't it?"

"Yes."

Perhaps she'd not said enough. "And how great you'll be working with Stella. You made a great team studying together. Of course she should work at the observatory. I mean even without what her dad does, there's her name and when I first saw her I thought how her skin was as velvety smooth as the night sky. I mean there are just so many signs this is right."

"Oh, I hadn't thought of that. Of course! Didn't I always say I'd find a sign to my future in the stars?"

Way to go, Heidi. Keep on like that and they'll ask you to be their matron of honour.

"Something like that, yes. So this is your job sorted out. What about other things?"

"What other things?"

"Oh, love... that sort of stuff." She was sure her face was the colour of Mars. "Will the answer to that be in the stars too?"

"I believe so, yes."

She still had a chance then; he hadn't already found his sign.

Heidi visited the library and borrowed an armful of reference books. With the aid of their charts she tried to find a constellation among her freckles. Even using a mirror the nearest she could manage was two thirds of Orion's Belt. That wouldn't convince anyone though as it was just two freckles near each other. Now, if she had three in a row... Heidi considered adding one as a tattoo but that wasn't likely to convince Carl either.

When Carl saw her borrowed books he said, "Got you interested at last have I?"

"Oh, I'm interested all right." She was of course but mostly with something a little more down to earth; him.

"It's better getting out and seeing them for real," Carl said.

"Too much light pollution around here," she said, repeating one of the few facts she remembered.

"Come to Scotland. We'll camp out somewhere really remote and watch the stars."

Somewhere all remote, just the two of them cosying up in a tent, sounded perfect. Sadly that wasn't what he meant. They were going with a whole bunch of geeky kids who formed the observatory's junior astronomy club, plus Professor Edwards and his daughter Stella.

Even after learning that and the fact she'd need to apply for CRB clearance and attend a first aid course, Heidi decided she couldn't back out. She not only agreed to go, but offered to do all the cooking too. Carl made it clear he really appreciated her help, which was something. She'd be able to show him what a good wife she could be for him.

Heidi did get to cosy up in a two person tent, but it was

Stella not Carl she shared it with. It didn't matter much though. After Heidi spent all day cooking and washing up and half the night star gazing, she was asleep the minute she crawled into her sleeping bag. Despite that she did enjoy herself.

The geeky kids reminded her of Carl at school and everyone's enthusiasm was infectious. It had been pretty cool to look through the telescope and see craters on the moon and Saturn's rings. By the fifth day Heidi could recognise and name dozens of stars and constellations and had impressed Carl with her culinary abilities.

On the last night the weather changed. It became cloudy and much cooler. As star gazing was out they made a campfire, told stories and toasted marshmallows on sticks over the flames. Carl sat close to Heidi as they watched the children's faces bright in the firelight.

"I'm so glad you came, Heidi."

"Me too."

"You didn't get much chance with the telescope though, what with keeping everyone going with hot chocolate. Maybe we could..." His words were cut short by a scream.

They ran over to discover it was Stella who was in pain, but the screaming was coming from a child who'd accidentally burned her with a stick left too long in the fire.

"Carl, you look after him. Everyone else get water."

Heidi repeatedly doused Stella's arm with cold water. It was difficult to see how much damage had been done, because of the poor light and the fact that Stella was wearing a thin synthetic jacket. It had melted and Heidi feared it was welded to her skin.

"It's not too bad," Stella said. "Doesn't hurt at all now

you've cooled it down."

Hoping that was true and the other girl wasn't putting on an incredibly brave face for the children, Heidi said, "Let's get into the tent and take a better look."

Carl and Professor Edwards took the children well away from the fire. She heard Carl saying they were going to have a quiz. Good; that would keep them occupied and happy.

Better lighting revealed that, although badly melted, the jacket wasn't stuck to Stella. It was burned through in a few spots but as Heidi poured on more water she saw even those areas lifted free of Stella's arm.

"I think this is ruined anyway, so it might be better if I cut it off you rather than pull it off."

"OK," Stella agreed.

Once Heidi had snipped around the shoulder with nail scissors the sleeve fell away, revealing raised specs in a pattern rather like a wobbly cross. It was an arrangement she'd seen before. "It looks just like a constellation," she told Stella.

The other girl laughed. "That's a nice idea. Thanks, Heidi."

"I'm not just trying to cheer you up, it really does. Cygnus, I think it is. See, those are the wings and that's the head."

"Well, would you look at that!" Stella said. It seemed the pattern that would be made by her tiny scars more than made up for a little pain and the loss of her jacket.

Heidi stared at Stella's arm. The girl shared Carl's passion and his work. She was clever, attractive and pleasant; even to Heidi who wasn't always very friendly towards her. She was the daughter of someone he greatly admired and now she would be permanently marked with a constellation.

"It's a sign," she whispered.

"A sign of what?" Stella asked.

"Oh nothing. Well, something Carl said once."

"Oh. Do you mean that the stars would show his path? He said something like that to me once. Oh, do you think this means...?"

"Knock, knock," Professor Edwards called.

"Come in, Dad," Stella replied. "Look, I'm fine thanks to Heidi."

"That's good news. Thank you, Heidi. Oh, Cygnus!"

Heidi sighed. No hope then that the significance of those dots would be lost on Carl.

"Stella, do you feel up to walking over and showing the kids you're OK?"

"Yes, I'm absolutely fine. I bet Peter feels bad. It wasn't really his fault you know."

"Come on then. You coming too, Heidi?"

"In a minute. I'll just tidy up in here and try to dry things out a bit."

When she joined the others, Carl took her to one side. "You were brilliant."

"Just glad I did that first aid course now."

"Bet Stella is too. My instinct was to pull the jacket off her. If I'd done that while it was still hot I might have caused a worse injury. As it is, I think she's quite pleased with Cygnus."

"I suppose you are too?"

"I'm glad she's not seriously hurt of course."

"It's your sign, Carl. Don't you see? You said there would be a sign in the stars. Stella's perfect for you isn't she?"

"Theoretically yes .. but she's not you, Heidi."

"Really?"

"Yes. I did think I'd get a sign until I saw Stella's arm. I like her a lot, but I don't love her. I like looking up at the stars, but I can't live among them."

"Earth is beautiful too. I think you'll like it down here."

"With you?"

"Of course with me."

As they kissed they heard a cheer. They looked up and saw the clouds had cleared to reveal a meteor shower. Heidi didn't make a wish as a dozen shooting stars fell to earth. She didn't need to, hers had just come true.

2. Butterflies And Moths

I've always been a moth. Quiet and plain, but possibly interesting if you look closely. That's what Sam did. I don't know why, but when I was drawn to him, as moths are said to be awestruck by the moon, he seemed attracted too.

There's a butterfly farm at the edge of town. It's a fancy conservation and study place, but locals call it the butterfly farm and often head there on cold grey days to enjoy brightly coloured insects, exotic plants, and tea and cake. That's what I was doing when I met Sam. Although I can't remember why I'd needed cheering up, I do know he did the trick.

"Come with me and watch the chrysalis hatching." He took my hand and led me to the warm, dark space. We watched in rapt wonder as the dull brown parcels revealed crumpled beauty which gradually expanded into colourful flight. Afterwards he offered to buy me a slice of cake. Lemon drizzle, if you want all the details.

I knew it wouldn't last. He was a student passing through; and me, I was a moth. We had a wonderful few months though and I had no regrets, not even after he'd gone and I felt new life flutter in my belly.

I didn't worry about breaking the news to my parents. They realised about the same time as I did that my bouts of sickness weren't just pre-exam nerves. They were surprised, my school friends and teachers too. Being a moth helped. I was too quiet and dull to be guilty of a sin I should be condemned for. My parents had me late in life and were pleased in some ways not to have a long wait for a grandchild. I didn't get many qualifications but I had an easy time of it. If the actual birth was hard, then I don't remember. No, that's not really true, but the pain was a tiny price to pay for the feelings which surged through me as my daughter was placed in my arms.

Ella was my beautiful butterfly. If I'd been dazzled by her father it was a blink of an eye at a passing moment's brightness, whereas my daughter was light. Light and beauty and joy. Of course I'm her mother and biased, but plenty of others noticed it too. Never once did she cause me trouble, or perhaps again I don't remember. There were the usual childhood illnesses and scraped knees, I suppose. She was an adventurer right from the start and trips to A&E for stitches or butterfly plasters to put her back together weren't a rare event, but I always knew she'd be OK.

Naturally I took her to the butterfly farm. She loved it even as a baby. Perhaps just because it was warm to start with, but soon she noticed the gorgeous winged creatures swooping past. One time, just after Ella started school, I saw a notice advertising for staff. Applying seemed an obvious step. I got the job. Nothing glamorous; making tea and washing cake plates. I loved it. Ella was happy to come in and wait for me after school, often bringing friends. Not that she waited in the tea rooms, it was always the butterflies she headed for.

Our garden at home became a wildlife haven. Ella helped me plant buddleia to attract peacocks, painted ladies and red admirals. Then, as she learned more, we allowed nettles to grow.

"The caterpillars need them to feed on, Mum," she explained.

Later we added food plants for holly blues and marsh fritillaries. That last was overly ambitious, but we were visited by many different species.

Ella was part buddleia bush herself, attracting bright friends and then young men. These fluttered round her and around me when they realised that, as well as saving them a large slice of the choicest cakes, I might introduce them to my beautiful daughter. Sometimes I did, if they seemed really nice. My daughter wasn't as easily dazzled as her mother.

She did well in her exams, then got a first class degree and the job she most wanted; research lepidopterist. She travelled the world studying the butterflies she loved. I was so proud of her. Proud of myself too every time I looked at her. She was beautiful, and not just in looks. Ella was sweet, talented and so much fun; and I'd produced her, helped to make her what she was.

There was my own quiet moth-like success too. I worked my way up to become manager. Not of the whole establishment of course, just the tea rooms. That was something though. More than might have been expected from a girl who got pregnant in school. The tea rooms thrived and contributed worthwhile funds to help retain butterfly habitats.

I couldn't help learning about butterflies and moths myself. I learned how fragile they are; easily harmed by the tiniest drift of chemical spray or slight change in the ecosystems on which they depend. And how strong; able to hibernate through harsh winters or travel on migrations of thousands of miles. I discovered not all moths are small and drab. The elephant hawk moth, for example, is big and colourful enough to rival those peacocks and red admirals we all love.

Ella continued to flit about the edges of my life, coming home as often as she could. She emailed and we chatted on Skype. Both of us were happy. Ella in her bright, beautiful butterfly way and me a quiet, contented moth. Mostly contented anyway. My parents were gone by then and I'd progressed as far as I could at work. I wasn't unhappy, but there was no bright light for me to eagerly circle as my forty-fifth birthday passed.

Not until Morton. He was a *morpho coerulescens*. That's an exotic species, chocolate brown when its wings are closed, but rich dazzling blue when they open for flight. If you didn't look closely you might mistake Morton for ordinary, but every now and then I'd catch a breathtakingly lovely smile, rivalling the most startling example of winged iridescence. He was brilliant in lots of ways, most of them the same as my daughter. But he could rest quietly like a moth, like me.

Morton made me laugh in a way I never had before unless Ella was home. Our friendship was no secret, but my deeper feelings were. He was a thirty-seven-year-old butterfly and I was an eight-years-older moth. We went for a drink or a meal now and then, as friends. That's how he'd intended the invitations I'm sure, and it's the way I accepted them.

Ella came home for a visit. My secret was no secret from her.

"Go for it, Mum!" she told me as though I too had shimmering wings to unfurl.

Morton saw me next to Ella. Although he noticed her beauty and welcomed her light shining on him, he wasn't dazzled. He wasn't blinded so as not to see the moth.

"I didn't realise you were Ella's mother," he said. He

explained how, through their work, he knew her. They'd collaborated on a couple of projects.

"Why should you? Jones isn't exactly an unusual surname and... I'm a moth."

"Yes, I rather think you are." He said it as though it was a good thing.

"She's a butterfly, my daughter."

"Oh yes, definitely. A *papilio thoas*." He pointed to a shimmering flutter of colour.

"Yes that's her and you're a *morpho coerulescens*."

"I am?" He looked thoughtful as he considered the comparison. I saw he liked it and then the moment he saw beyond it to the reason. My secret was out.

I ran away. Not literally, moths just quietly float away leaving you still looking at the light. I took myself back to the kitchen and avoided him for the rest of the day.

That night I stared at my face in the mirror. It was still that quiet little moth who looked back. I hadn't changed much; one good thing about not having beauty to fade. It was the same face Sam had seen and he'd been attracted, hadn't he? I was the moth, but it was on me he'd briefly chosen to shine his light. And there was Ella. I'd produced that magnificent creature, but she'd left behind more than a shrivelled discarded chrysalis.

Back at work I sought out Morton. No all right, I didn't. I was still a moth, but at least I didn't fly away when he came looking for me.

"We didn't finish our conversation," he said.

If I'd had wings they'd have fluttered as though disturbed by a breeze. As I had none, I stood still and stared at the cake counter.

"Come with me." He took my hand and led me to a display area much as Sam had done all those years before. Morton didn't show me bright butterflies. He showed me moths.

"That one, the *scopula ornata*. That's you."

It was plain cream. Rather nice looking with the lacy edges and moonlight shimmer to its wings and, from what Morton told me, interesting in its way. I saw the delicate creature reflected in his eyes and knew that really was how he saw me. As a moth, and he thought that was a good thing. I remembered what Ella had told me about the difference between moths and butterflies. There isn't one, not really. Butterflies often fold their wings when at rest, some don't. Most moths fly at night, but not all. The creatures themselves don't know these rules and sometimes the divisions are blurred.

"I was wondering..." Morton said. "If we could get a coffee together? Not here I don't mean and not just as friends..."

I'd had a coffee with Sam once. That led to something beautiful, my beloved Ella. She'd flown away on her own, but my wings had never been tried. Maybe this moth could learn to fly in daylight. To open my wings to the light and allow their delicate colour to shimmer.

"Yes. I'd like that."

3. Climbing Mountains

Tasha leant over Craig's shoulder and looked at the magazine he was reading.

"Thinking of going mountaineering?" she asked.

Craig flinched. He'd been so interested in the article he hadn't noticed her arrival. Looking down at the photograph of Kilimanjaro, rising icy and majestic from the African plains, Craig recalled reading about the difficulties faced during a climb and the exhilaration experienced at the summit.

Tasha flipped over a page. A picture of Everest and an inset of a mountaineer were revealed. Alongside was yet another article describing the sense of achievement and complete freedom the man felt after climbing to the top of the world. Craig would never know that feeling.

"So, are you thinking of having a go?" Tasha asked again.

Craig shook his head. He could have tried explaining why climbing Everest wasn't a popular sport amongst wheelchair users, but he'd be wasting his breath. Tasha always acted as though she couldn't see his chair, or the crutches he could drag himself about on for short periods. Tasha's belief he could do anything had often spurred him on to achieve things he and his family had thought were impossible. Thanks to Tasha's encouragement, Craig had a job and could drive an adapted car. He loved her for all of that, but sometimes Craig got annoyed with Tasha's inability to face his limitations.

"You could do that," Tasha said, pointing to the picture of

another man on a mountain top. "All mountaineers need help; you'd not be any different."

Of course, he'd be different. He wasn't like the explorers he admired.

"Great idea, I'll nip down to Millets and get some karabiners and ice picks, shall I, whilst you book the flights to base camp?" he snapped.

"Don't be stupid, Craig," she yelled after him as he wheeled away from her.

Tasha left and didn't come back. Why had she done that? Tasha never shouted or stormed out of the room, no matter what he said. She normally called to apologise the day after a row. Craig checked his messages every hour; nothing.

"Why don't you call her?" his mum asked.

Great; another person who thought a few sweet words could make everything all right. They couldn't, nothing could fix his legs and turn him into a man who deserved Tasha's love. She'd see that one day, until then he must try not to love her.

"What's the point? It's never going to work out between us," he told his mum.

"Only because you keep putting obstacles in the way."

He knew the arguments were usually his fault. He got frustrated at his inability to do things other people took for granted.

"It's part of me, Mum. If she can't accept it, she'll never really love me. I want her to understand that my crippled legs are as important as my achievements."

"She does, love. She just prefers to see the things you can do. For instance, Tasha probably thinks you're capable of dialling her number and saying you're sorry for shouting. I suppose she'd be wrong though, you're just a poor crippled boy who can't do nothing."

He moved back in his chair as though she'd slapped him. When he was unhappy, that was exactly how he felt, but how could his mum say it?

"Mum, that's not fair, you don't know what it's like."

"I don't know? You think it's easy for a mother to watch her son's legs wither so's he can hardly walk? Let me tell you, it isn't."

"I know, you've been great."

"Helping you learn to use crutches and a wheelchair wasn't the hardest bit. That was watching you sit and watch the other kids play football, or ride their bikes. I felt so helpless, knowing I couldn't do anything about it."

Craig hung his head. He'd known it had been hard having the house adapted and taking him to doctors and caring for him. He'd not noticed how his problems had hurt her.

His mum put her hand on his shoulder. "Things got better when Tasha moved next door. She got you interested in life, made you focus on what you could do."

Craig wiped his eyes and blew his nose. Without the support of his parents and Tasha, he'd probably have given up all thought of a fulfilling life. They'd done so much for him. Sometimes he wished they hadn't; they'd just given him false hope.

"I owe her a lot. She was a great friend when we were kids, but she can't see it's different now. She thinks we'll get married and live happily ever after."

"Isn't that what you want? You can't tell me you don't love her."

"It's what I want, but it's not fair to her."

"It's not fair for you to make her decisions for her. She knows her own mind."

"She thinks she does. What happens when she suddenly realises I can't be the man she wants me to be."

"Don't be stupid, Craig."

He thumped the arm of his chair, he was getting fed up with hearing those words. He wasn't stupid, he was disabled and those closest to him didn't understand.

He tried again to explain. "You remember she persuaded me to go to the college's end of year dance?"

"That was two years ago."

"I keep thinking about that. I saw other blokes dancing with their girlfriends. Right then, all I wanted, was to be able to hold Tasha in my arms and move with the music. Stupidly I told her that."

"Why is that stupid?" his mum asked.

"Because she dragged me onto the floor. For a couple of minutes it was great. With Tasha for support, I could stay upright and I had a brilliant excuse to hold her really tight. We didn't dance properly, just swayed about a bit, but that was OK too, because it was what everyone else did."

"So, where's the problem?"

"That came when the music stopped. My legs were like marshmallow, I couldn't walk and someone brought my chair. As Tasha wheeled me off the dance floor, people started clapping."

"Craig, that was your college friends. You've made too much of this."

"They clapped, Mum," Craig shouted. "People don't clap when normal people dance."

"You got to dance with the girl you love and you're angry

that people where pleased for you. All that mattered to you was whether you walked off the floor or someone pushed you. I bet that made Tasha feel great." His mum took a deep breath and continued more gently, "I'd known your dad three years before he plucked up the courage to ask me to dance. All our friends cheered us when we took to the floor."

"That's different though. When Dad married you he walked you back down the aisle, you didn't have to push him. You didn't have to check the honeymoon suite had disabled access and an adapted bathroom."

"It's time you faced up to facts, love."

Craig blinked. "Me?"

"Yes, accept you're a normal bloke who's got dodgy legs. Accept you've got to learn to trust other people and risk getting your heart broken if you want a normal life."

His mum didn't tell him not be stupid for a second time, he was beginning to work that out for himself. He called Tasha. "I'm sorry," he said.

"That's OK."

"It's not OK. I can't climb Everest on crutches, but that was no reason to shout at you."

"I'm glad you've decided against it, I was thinking of somewhere a lot less high and preferably a fair bit warmer."

He smiled, of course she was. She knew what he was capable of. The band had been playing a rock song when he asked her to dance; she'd waited for a smoochy number before taking to the floor.

"So we just need to find an incredibly small mountain, in the med that has wheelchair access?"

"Exactly."

Craig laughed.

"So, will you do it? If I found a mountain like that, would you climb it with me?"

The woman never gave up. He paused; taking a holiday together was a big step. There wasn't a mountain like that, but he'd be agreeing to the idea of moving their relationship on. "OK."

Three months later, they'd taken a taxi to the airport. Craig had done some research and made the bookings on-line. Ignoring his pride and declaring his disability had made things easier, they were taken right to the plane on a special buggy. They were met on arrival and quickly assisted through customs and onto the transfer bus. The hotel was great, they had a ground floor suite and everything was accessible.

It was all going fine until Tasha said they should see some of the countryside and wanted to hire a car. They couldn't get one modified for Craig to drive. He almost yelled not to bother at the booking clerk, but he saw Tasha's unhappy face. She wanted to explore, it was unfair to deny her the chance just because he felt inadequate. He insisted on paying, that way he felt he was making a contribution to the journey.

Once they were travelling through fabulous Spanish scenery, he knew he'd done the right thing. Tasha looked so happy. As the winding road climbed higher, he felt he was rising above his problems. They wouldn't go away, but perhaps with a few compromises Craig could have a decent life.

"So where are we going?" he asked Tasha.

She grinned. "Nearly there."

He guessed she must have got directions to a good vantage point.

"Here we are. Out you get."

He pulled himself out of the car, leant on his crutches and looked around. The view really was spectacular. They were on one end of a sweep of rocky mountain tops. The clear air was scented with pine. Craig couldn't hear anything except his own breathing. In front of them was a huge flattish piece of rock. It jutted out, above the lush green valley far below.

"That's it," she pointed along the length of rock. "Our mountain."

Craig laughed. She was right, if they walked to the edge and looked out, it really would feel as though they were on top of a mountain.

Tasha put her hand on his arm. "Craig?" She looked worried.

"This is brilliant, Tasha, thank you. A proper mountain for me to climb, I can't believe it. You say I can do anything, I can't you know, but you sure can."

"About that." She looked like she might cry.

He touched her cheek. "What?"

"They said it's safe enough to walk out there."

"I'm not worried, you're right this is something I can do. It looks lovely and smooth."

"That's the trouble, it's slippery they said. It'd be dangerous to go right to the end in case we slipped and..." Tasha stopped talking.

He waited.

"Craig, you could do it, I know you could, but..."

"But?"

"I'd be worried. You might slip. I'd feel better if you were in the chair."

She didn't look at him, so she didn't see his smile. Craig opened the boot of the car and began to assemble his wheelchair.

Tasha took them as close to the edge as she dared. They held hands but didn't speak. They looked out over the valley for a long time. As the sun touched the edge of the mountain opposite and stained the sky with jewel bright colour, they kissed.

"Thanks, Tasha," he said.

"No, thank you, this was your idea and you paid. All I've done is drive."

"You made it possible for me to climb a mountain."

"I'm sorry. About the chair, I..."

"I'm on top of a mountain with the girl I love. What does it matter if I walk back down, or I'm pushed in a chair?"

"It doesn't matter to me. You must know that by now."

"Yes, I know that. I know there are some things I won't ever be able to do, but that with your help there's a lot I can achieve. There's one thing I don't know though."

"Really, go on then, surprise me."

"I don't know if you'll marry me?"

4. Head To Toe

Andy tried not to stare at Sandra's legs as she passed his desk. She was perfect all over, but her legs were undoubtedly her best feature. Neat knees, trim calves, blemish-free skin and never a trace of stubble.

As he watched, the legs turned around. Andy blushed as Sandra asked if he'd had a good weekend.

"Yes, thanks. I went to see that new Johnny Depp film with my brother."

"Me too. Well, I went with my sister, not your brother. Brilliant wasn't it?"

As they discussed the plot, he discovered they'd both read the book and had the same tastes in literature. From previous conversations he knew they enjoyed the same music and food. Never once had she mentioned a boyfriend. He hoped that was for the same reason he'd never mentioned a girlfriend – there wasn't one.

While they talked, he kept his gaze firmly above her neckline on her nice, neat blonde hair. It helped that she constantly fiddled with it, smoothing it down, then fluffing it up. He was pleased there were no darker roots showing – he hated that. Andy sighed. Who was he to dislike minor imperfections in others when so far from perfect himself?

Sandra returned to her own desk. Everything between her sensible hair and dainty feet was perfect, and not just on the outside. She was one of the pleasantest and kindest people he'd ever met. She was patient with new staff, organised birthday gifts and visited sick colleagues. If anyone had a problem it was Sandra who helped them through it. She'd have helped him deal with his if she hadn't been the very last person he wanted to know about it.

Sandra again passed close to Andy's desk. She dropped a pencil, topped with a fluffy duck. Was that deliberate?

"I sometimes eat my lunch by the pond," she said as she patted at her hair. "I'm just as clumsy then, but instead of dropping ducks, I drop crumbs for them."

Was she saying their little chats were a few crumbs she was prepared to offer him?

No, he must be wrong. She wouldn't be cruel even if she did know about his problem. Not that she could. Andy took great care nobody did.

Andy was delighted when their boss suggested they work together on a project. Sandra seemed pleased too.

Their first combined presentation was such a success it gave Andy confidence. "That went well, I think?" he said to Sandra. "You really impressed them with your marketing pitch."

"Yes and you reassured them perfectly about supply and distribution. We make a great team."

"We do. I hope we'll work together again." He'd thought he was being too pushy half-way through the sentence, but was pleased to see her smile and nod.

"All that talking has made me thirsty," Sandra said.

They were walking towards the canteen, but Andy saw an opportunity. He could suggest they go for a drink as though he was inviting her out. If she reacted favourably, maybe he'd eventually build up confidence to ask her out for real.

"Sandra, er, shall we, I mean would you like to go for a drink?"

"Did you mean grab a coffee from the canteen now, or go for a glass of wine later?"

Andy blushed.

"Because both sound good." She blushed too.

Modesty was another of her good qualities, but how could she really doubt he'd want to take her out?

"Great, then we'll do both, shall we?" he managed to stutter.

To his amazement, nothing went wrong over coffee and Sandra agreed to join him in a local bar for a drink after work.

They carried their glasses to a quiet corner, fussed about getting seated, said 'cheers' and took a sip. Sandra twiddled her hair. Andy shuffled his feet. They looked away. Looked back.

Andy opened his mouth to speak just as Sandra said, "I thought I'd put my big foot in it."

"You thought what?" he was startled into snapping.

"Suggesting the wine. I worried you just saw me as a friend sort of, not someone... oh dear, I mean..." She scratched her head.

"Sandra, I think you're lovely. Perfect. I'd like very much for us to go out together."

"That's wonderful, although I'm not perfect."

He reached over to take the hand which was still fiddling with her hair. "To me you are."

They went to dinner a few nights later, to the cinema at the weekend and ate their lunch together by the pond every day.

One afternoon, as Sandra reached up to get a file from a

shelf, a colleague called, "Pity for you and Andy this office is open plan and we don't have a stationery cupboard for you to disappear into."

Sandra pulled down the file she wanted. As she did, a stapler was dislodged and very narrowly missed hitting her head.

"What idiot put that there?" she demanded.

"Keep your hair on, Sandra, it was just an accident," someone said.

"That's it, laugh. I could have been seriously hurt, but everyone thinks health and safety is just a joke apparently."

Andy, and everyone else, was surprised at this flash of temper. It must have been the shock. Had the stapler hit her it would have been very painful.

Even as he mentally explained her outburst, Andy wondered if it was to do with people guessing about their relationship. She soon proved that wasn't the case.

"Sorry," she mumbled to the girl she'd shouted at. "You're right about the stationery cupboard. Guess we'll have to make our romance open plan." She sauntered over to Andy and kissed him.

The boss arrived just in time to see Sandra embrace Andy. "So, it's official with you two is it?"

They both nodded – and both blushed.

"Good. I wanted to give you some reward for the great job you did with those presentations and something has just come up. A client has offered me a stay on a Greek island. Wonderful weather, fabulous beach, what do you say?"

Andy was horrified; she'd see his feet and he wasn't ready. He refused straight away. Sandra also declined, but seemed sad. She must think he didn't want to go on holiday with her.

He did, very much, but not before he'd warned her about the flap of skin between each of his toes. Somehow, he'd never got around to telling her that his feet looked alarmingly like those of a seagull.

She was still there in front of him, scratching at her head. Everyone else had vanished.

Andy said, "It's not that I don't want to be with you. It's just... Can we go out this weekend? We'll go anywhere you like." Or at least, anywhere he could keep his socks on.

"Andy, I think we should talk."

"Right, yes."

"Not now."

No, of course not. She was too nice to dump him at work.

"Perhaps on Friday?"

Good thinking. That would give him the weekend to try to pull himself together.

"Come round to my place. There's an Italian restaurant quite close, we could go there later. That's if you still want to."

So she wasn't going to dump him? He could have danced down the corridor, except the sad look was still on her face. Not sad, worried. She hadn't wanted to go on the holiday either. Maybe she worried it was rushing things. Andy was happy to take things slowly, really get to know her before explaining about his webbed toes.

Or maybe she was ill, or needed help with something. Whatever it was, he'd be there for her and she'd still be perfect to him.

He had a momentary pang of guilt as he realised he'd actually feel better if she had a problem he could help with. First though he needed to sort out his own problem – not the toes, but his inferiority complex about them. Sandra was a lovely girl, kind. If she cared for him, it would take more than a bit of extra skin to put her off.

Friday evening, he took a huge bouquet of flowers to Sandra's flat.

"I'll put the flowers in water." She pointed to an open doorway. "Make yourself comfortable."

Andy sat himself on her sofa, then almost without thinking pulled off his shoes and socks. He stared at his ugly feet until he noticed her perfect toes right in front of them.

"I wanted to tell you," he mumbled.

"Tell me what?"

"About my feet." He raised one and splayed his toes.

"Oh! You've got funny feet."

"Yes." He smiled. She was right, he had funny feet. It wasn't the horrible affliction he sometimes thought, he just had feet that were a bit funny looking. "You don't mind?"

"Why would I? I love you from your head to your cute toes."

Something soft and silky descended to cover his bare feet. It looked just like Sandra's hair. He looked up, taking in her lovely legs, trim figure in a red cotton dress, and pretty face. There was more face on show than usual as her neat blonde hair no longer framed it. Sandra was bald.

"I have alopecia."

Andy nodded, it explained a lot.

"Do you mind?"

"Why would I? Sandra, I love you from your boringly normal toes to the top of your perfect, naked head."

5. Cloud Dragons

Ugly dark clouds gathered overhead. Sasha wasn't sure if it was rain or tears sliding down her face.

They'd had a row. It had been so silly; that they'd rowed at all, but also the reason for it.

"It's no good you saying I need imagination! This place is a dump and no amount of wishful thinking will change that," she'd complained to Tim.

"Wishful thinking won't, but hard work and paint will."

Tim was good with paint, but even his artistic talents, which could turn blank canvas into a fairy-tale woodland, must be defeated by this dingy, dirty depressing box of bricks.

"Petrol and a box of matches would be better," Sasha said.

He'd laughed, then started to explain how stripping off the navy paper with its outsize pattern would transform the claustrophobic hallway. "A pale gold background, to bring in a touch of sunshine, and perhaps delicate sprays of tiny flowers. And if we got rid of the door and lifted this lino and the carpet on the stairs, to reveal the pale wood beneath, it would make it into one open area."

The way he talked they'd soon have it looking as good as Leanna's place, but Sasha wanted somewhere which was attractive in reality, not just in Tim's imagination.

Sasha should have been excited that her boyfriend wanted to buy a house with her. That was a good thing. She would have been pleased if it wasn't for her half-sister. Leanna was happily married to Paul and had a house much nicer than the one Tim had taken her to look at could ever be.

Leanna had always been a few steps ahead. She was Daddy's first, most loved, child. He'd said it wasn't true and that he loved them both just as much, but in that case why did he keep going back to see her when he was supposed to live with Mum and Sasha?

At school she'd always felt in the shadow of her older, more creative half-sister. Sasha passed her maths tests, but it was Leanna who starred in every school play, whose voice rang out in assembly. Sasha carefully worked towards a proper career, Leanna just sang. No. Not just sang, she dreamed and laughed and captivated the hearts of all those she met. Even Sasha's. She'd loved to hear Leanna sing and talk about her plans.

Sasha got a sensible job in a bank, but the nice sensible men she met there sat entranced as Leanna sang, it seemed, everywhere they went.

Tim was different. He heard not a siren call, but only the songs she sang.

"I'm a dreamer like your sister," he said after a barbecue at Leanna and Paul's. "And like her, I need someone practical in my life."

Paul and Sasha were the practical ones who dashed round taking in cushions and the remains of lunch when it looked like rain. Tim and Leanna laughed up at the stormy skies trying to guess which cloud dragon would be the first to spit out a fiery breath of lightning and hurl rain onto the mortals below.

For a while Sasha too had dreamed. She'd imagined Tim down on one knee asking her to marry him. She'd looked forward to a happy future with him and forgotten her jealousy of Leanna. But her dreams had proved to be just wishful thinking. Her dreamer didn't love her as much as Leanna's practical man loved his wife.

Then had come the house viewing. Tim had tried to get her to see it as he did, but all Sasha could see, when she let her imagination drift, was the cheerful, cosy building Leanna called home. She'd left, slamming the door behind her.

It wasn't until she sank onto a bench in the park that Sasha realised the darkness and angry thunder wasn't all in her mind. It was going to rain. She looked up and, through the blur of her tears, for a moment the clouds looked like dragons.

"Sasha, I'm sorry." Tim stood a little way off.

She'd allowed her imagination to run away with her and was disappointed as a result. It wasn't Tim's fault. Sasha tried to explain her dissatisfaction with the house, as her sadness over their relationship was too painful to talk about.

"All I could see was Leanna's place."

"You did?" He sounded confused.

"Yes." And then she really did. The reason she'd been reminded of her sister's home was that the two were similar. Not the same, but with imagination, paint and yes, an awful lot of hard work, it could be just as nice. Her dreamer had seen that and she should have trusted him.

Tim wasn't like her, but they complemented each other. Sasha wasn't like Leanna either, but that didn't mean she must try to compete. It was Paul whom Sasha had most in common with. He'd got hold of his dreamer; not with hoping but with simple, sensible action. So could she.

Sasha took Tim's hand and led him to the shelter of a tree just as the first raindrops splattered onto the dry earth.

"Will you marry me?" she asked.

He pulled her close and kissed her. "Yes, yes of course." Tim stepped back, pulled something from his pocket and handed it to her.

"What's this?"

"Something I've dreamed of giving you... Dreams aren't enough but between us we've got more than that. You're the practical one, open it and see."

It wasn't lightning but the headlights from a passing car which made the diamond of the ring sparkle, but the effect was the same.

Tim slipped the ring onto her finger. He kissed her again.

"We'd better go back into the house, those cloud dragons of yours are going to get really busy any minute."

"You can see the dragons?" Tim asked.

"No, but I know they're there."

6. A Perfect Match

Hannah didn't object to internet dating in principle; it was using a site recommended by her big sister that bothered her. She remembered the sporty guy Juliet introduced her to. He'd barely stirred from his armchair because he watched every game, race and match. Then there'd been the history enthusiast who was antique himself. Juliet admitted she'd 'met' them through e-loves.

"Please don't, Jules. I'm capable of contacting likely prospects myself."

"Go on then," Juliet replied, passing over the details. "This site is really good. You chat online before you even see their picture, so you get to know them first."

"Then discover they're aged 108?"

"That was my fault for not checking."

Hannah registered, but only to stop Juliet making further arrangements on her behalf. Monday morning she logged on and scrolled through the list of matches produced. She'd just read Mysterious Mr T's profile when she saw Mitchell skulking into the office. By the time the boss reached her desk the computer screen showed the monthly accounts forecast. She didn't suppose he was fooled that had held her attention since nine, but there was nothing he could do armed with suspicion alone.

When the coast was clear, Hannah logged back onto e-loves. Mr T's profile status showed he'd arranged a date with Girlie Shirley. He'd forever remain a mystery to Hannah. All those she'd looked at earlier were now either engaged in electronic chatting or arranging dates. Maybe she'd received messages herself?

No, only a welcome from the site administrator. Maybe her name was the problem? Most screen names were amusing, or gave hints of personality or appearance. She'd listed herself simply as Hannah. Hopeful Hannah sounded desperate, mousey-locks hardly inspiring and Leo Lady rather a man-eater. She'd probably better avoid anything involving her surname of Ramsbottom. Eventually she settled for Happy Hannah.

Mitchell was on the warpath again so Hannah couldn't get back onto the site until lunchtime. She was glad she'd taken to bringing in sandwiches to avoid the slick of spread the deli slathered over everything no matter how often she asked for just a little. Hannah placed her sandwich on a serviette so the extra cucumber wouldn't make a mess. Ignoring her book on Anne Boleyn she took a large bite of tuna on brown and logged onto e-loves. Still no messages. Her expression belied the nickname she'd chosen.

She scrolled through matches and came across Happy Harry. His profile claimed he was her age, lived locally, ran half marathons and was fascinated by the Tudors. He sounded perfect. Ping. Her computer announced a message from him.

'Do you think we could be happy together?'

'Maybe. Coincidence over the names – I've only just picked mine.'

'Me too!'

They exchanged messages until one, then Harry said he must return to work.

'Be home @6.30. Will log in then and hope to chat.'

Never had an afternoon dragged so much. Fortunately Mitchell didn't try his usual trick of calling her into his office to discuss some boring point just before five, so she left on time.

She and Harry chatted all evening, even watching a film together by sitting with their laptops in front of their televisions. They worked in similar offices, both had one older, slightly bossy, sibling and passed their driving tests at the second attempt. They liked camping. Neither liked rap music, junk mail or celery.

When she joked about being out of chocolate biscuits and said he'd have to have custard creams he emailed a picture of his keyboard surrounded by crumbs saying she should have faxed it over. Hannah giggled; his sense of humour was as daft as her own.

Before they said goodnight, they agreed to chat the following lunchtime. 'And maybe we can think of something to do together this weekend?' he added.

When he logged on at lunchtime, not a second before, Hannah said his office manager must be even more of a slave driver than hers.

'You might be right. You'd best ask my staff.'

'Oops!'

'It's OK – but you'll see I can hardly chat to you during working hours then tell my staff off for wasting time on Facebook or whatever.'

'Suppose not. Bet you're not as strict as my boss. If I'm thirty seconds late back from lunch or try to leave by five he wants to know why.'

'You should still be at your desk working at five, not have your coat on and be heading for the door, young woman!!!'

Hannah stuck her tongue out at the screen then smiled as his next message appeared.

'If fraternising with a member of management isn't against your principles, will you come for a drink on Friday?'

'Might be able to bring myself to do that – even if it's just so I can try to persuade you to be fair to your staff.' She pressed 'send' and immediately panicked he might not realise she was teasing.

Fortunately his reply arrived swiftly and he didn't seem annoyed. 'You won't get the chance, I'll be too busy educating you on the pressures of management. Or maybe we can talk about something other than work?'

'Good plan. Let's start now.'

The time flashed by and soon Happy Harry said, 'Lunch over. Got to go – chat tonight?'

That evening Hannah thanked her sister for suggesting e-loves and told her about Happy Harry.

"Fantastic! Just remember to follow the rules about meeting in a public place, letting someone know where you're going... Talking of that, I'm meeting Cuddly Monkey for a drink on Friday in Rumours bar at seven."

"Cuddly Monkey? You're kidding me!"

"It's just a nickname."

"Probably means he's twenty stone and way too touchy-feely."

"Well, Happy Harry probably has a warped sense of humour. Although, come to think of it, that'd make him perfect for you."

"I think he is, we've got loads in common. Just wait until Monkey Features discovers you like making clothes from old curtains to wear while you sing along to *The Sound of*

Music."

"Actually, he said that sounds like a laugh."

"You admitted you're involved with Amateur Dramatics and he's still interested?"

"He said his company could do us a good deal printing the programmes."

"Good grief; he's your Mister Right!"

Hannah suggested to Harry they meet in Rumours bar at seven. Not only would it reassure Juliet her little sister was safe, Hannah might get a look at Monkey Man. Over the next few days, Hannah and Harry's chats showed her how her office etiquette must seem from Mitchell's point of view. She made efforts to be a better employee as well as giving Harry a few tips to improve the life of his staff.

The bar was almost empty when Hannah arrived. No sign of Harry, or Juliet come to that. Hannah checked her watch and discovered she was actually early. She chose a seat where she could watch everyone as they came in. E-loves suggested they agreed a way to recognise each other at their first meeting and she and Harry decided to wear something orange in honour of their favourite fruit. Hannah's black and gold print dress was the closest she'd managed but they knew each other so well that it wouldn't be a problem.

Two women came in, followed by a blond man; definitely not Harry. The next man looked about right but went straight over to the women and greeted them enthusiastically. Then Mitchell walked in. With horror she realised he broadly matched the description Harry had given her. No! Surely it couldn't be? He was wearing a peach coloured shirt though, which was as close to orange as her dress.

Mitchell walked straight over to her. "Good evening, Hannah."

"Hello, Mitchell."

"Er. Right, well can I get you a drink?" He looked as confused as she felt.

"Thanks, a rum and Coke would be good."

No sooner had he turned away to head for the bar than Juliet arrived.

"Disaster, Hannah!"

"I'll say! Do you have any idea who my date is?"

"Can't be as bad as mine who's waiting outside."

"What's wrong with that? Maybe he wants to be exactly on time."

"It's not the timing, it's the man. He's a right weirdo. I see him most lunchtimes and the fuss he makes in the sandwich shop. No butter, extra salad yada yada."

"And what's wrong with that?"

"It's as annoying as waiting for you to finish faffing around in the kitchen! And that's not all, he carries the most tedious looking history books... Oh hello, you must be Happy Harry."

Hannah, wondering which period of history interested the man, swung round to see Mitchell holding her drink.

"No... Cuddly Monkey."

Juliet squealed and introduced herself as DohRaeMe. "Sorry, Hannah. That means weirdo could be your date."

The man, wearing a marigold pinned to his lapel, looked around uncertainly. He was the same height and build as Harry claimed to be and had the sort of dark curly hair Hannah liked.

Juliet continued, "I've messed up again; I'd never have suggested e-loves if I'd known he was registered..."

"Then it's a jolly good thing you didn't know."

Hannah walked over and introduced herself to the new arrival. He broke into a broad grin, proving the name Happy Harry was entirely appropriate.

She remembered his first comment to her had been to ask if she thought they could be happy together; she believed they could.

7. Treasure Hunt

My life resembles a badly clichéd movie. I'm so great at my temporary job I'm begged to stay permanently. I advance to management, get a company car and huge salary. I'm so pretty the office heart-throb is always pursuing me. I turn him down as I'm engaged to a rock star. Then I wake and it was all a dream.

The reality is less good. I'm standing in for a lady who's on maternity leave. She brought her baby in yesterday, saying she couldn't wait to return. I don't have friends here. They're pleasant enough, but that's just good manners.

I didn't want to come on this silly team building day. No one really wants me here. If I'd stayed away I wouldn't have been missed. They had to invite me, everyone is attending. They could hardly leave the temp running the office.

The sad thing is I don't really want the dream. I just want a steady job, preferably with some prospects. I would like friends, and I'd like to get asked out by, well by almost anyone really.

Packed lunches are handed out as we board the coach. Should I take a look now so I have something to look forward to? Better wait in case the contents are disappointing. I expect these sandwiches are going to be the highlight of the day.

Why didn't I just take a day off? This is going to be awful. I don't know any jokes. I am too shy to start conversations, or contribute much to anyone else's. I don't drink, I'm boring.

"What star sign are you, Sylvie?" Alice, the section manager, asks.

"Capricorn."

"Ooh same as Linda. Listen up Lind, this one's for you too. 'Life has not been living up to your expectations lately.'"

"When does it ever?" Linda, the boss' PA replies.

"Do you want to hear this?"

"Go on then," Linda says. She sounds martyred and gives a huge sigh, an affect ruined by her grin.

"OK where was I? 'Dreams alone are not enough. With the help of like-minded friends you can turn dreams to reality. A money worry will be eased on Wednesday.'"

"Budge up. I want to sit with Sylvie," Linda says. "I had this dream about Prince Harry last night and obviously she can make it come true."

There's a lot of laughter.

"He will probably sue the paper if that happens," Alice says.

"Oi, cheeky."

Linda does come and sit with me. I'd thought one of the management team would be forced to do that, so I didn't feel ignored. This is an improvement; Linda has always been kind to me. She's funny, and very talkative. We can chat all the way without me doing more than look interested and nod occasionally.

"So will you introduce me to Prince William, Sylvie?"

"Of course, next time he pops round I'll give you a call." I hope I don't sound sarcastic. I want to join in the game but don't know how.

"So got any dreams I can help with?"

I want to shout, 'Yes! Be my friend. Persuade management to give me a full-time job. Help me be confident like you.' I just smile.

"Go on, you can tell me. Can't keep a secret of course, but I'd try to help."

"Thanks."

"Want me to fix you up with Nigel?"

'Yes please,' I yell, but silently. He isn't interested in me. He smiles, but doesn't say much. Yet another dream that evaporates when exposed to reality.

"No? I suppose the Rowan Atkinson look doesn't appeal to everyone. Anyway you've got everything sorted haven't you?"

"Not everything."

"How can I help?"

"You could accidentally type up a contract in my name and slip it under Mr Glaston's pen when he's not concentrating."

"You want to stay on then?"

I nodded.

"Thought you temps liked flitting from job to job. Have you applied to stay?"

"No."

"Then it sounds like you need an application form slipped under your pen."

Nigel is handing out plastic cups and filling them from a jug of Pimm's.

"Not for me, I don't drink."

"Not even one?"

"No. Sorry to be boring."

"That's OK, leaves more for the rest of us."

Nigel scoops out some chopped fruit and an ice cube. He tops the cup up with lemonade and hands it to me.

"There you go, tiger. If you get legless on that I'll personally carry you round all day."

"Think I'll be alright with this." I briefly wonder if he would be likely to carry out this promise, if so I'd gladly take Linda's drink and down it in one. On balance, I think I'd better not risk it.

"Aw shame." He winks and the people around us laugh. Not at me I realise, but at the joke. I smile happily at him, proud of myself, a potentially embarrassing social situation and I coped.

Names are being drawn for the teams. Simon's name is called and everyone cheers. He's the guy, played by Tom Cruise, who'd be pestering me for dates if this was still the cinematic dream sequence.

"Pick me, Simon," Linda calls. I bet Dawn French could portray her enthusiasm really well.

 Pretty soon half the coach are chanting her words.

"No, no it doesn't work like that," explains Nigel.

"We don't want it to be like the old school games teams where you stand depressed at the back, just knowing you are going to be picked last."

So I hadn't been the only one to feel like that?

Mr Glaston is drawn as leader of team two. There is a cheer from him and a groan from the rest.

"There'll be no slackers in my team," he declares, shaking his finger at us.

If we didn't know him better we'd have thought he was serious. We know he wants everyone to have fun today. He's a popular boss. When I have spoken to him he's been kind, never intimidating. That shows how good he is with people when you consider I'm often nervous asking for my bus ticket when I don't have the exact change.

Another cheer greets the selection of the third team leader. I don't catch the name. A lady from accounts is then drawn for Simon's team. General comments about being alright for beer money are made. Alice is picked to join Mr Glaston. Wolf whistles and laughter greet this, not helped by Mr Glaston waggling his eyebrows at her. Alice is due to retire next year, but she still blushes and giggles like a schoolgirl who has just bumped into the lower sixth rugby captain outside the headmistress's office.

Nigel's name is the next to be drawn out of the bag.

"Yeah, I'm with you, Sylvie."

He nudges me gently. I don't mind the nudge but my expression must be strange.

"I just meant that I'm in your team."

"Mine?"

"Didn't you hear? You were picked as leader for team three. I reckon this is going to be fun."

"But that can't be right. Why would it be me?"

"Luck of the draw."

"But everyone cheered."

"Well yes. That's good surely? Means they like you."

People cheered for me? It's just high spirits, but perhaps it means I'm accepted. They consider me to be as good as the others whose names are being called.

"You're absolutely right. This is going to be fun," I say, half convincing myself it's true.

By the time we reach the Thames Embankment, the names have all been called and the Pimm's is just a sweet memory. Lager, wine and fruit juice are distributed and we eat our lunch sat on the warm grass with the Tate Modern behind us. The river and passers-by give us plenty to look at. Some of the group go for a quick look round the gallery.

"It was free to go in and I still wanted my money back."

"I'm going to send in my desk jotter, the doodles and coffee rings are better than what's in there."

"There was a rubbish bin, dunno if it was to use or if it was an exhibit."

Each team leader is given a padded envelope. Inside is a list of tasks and a disposable camera. Each of the leaders gives our mobile numbers to the others. Simon actually asked for my number, does that count as a dream coming true?

"Just give me the prize now and save yourselves the humiliation of defeat," is his next comment.

"Oh no; I don't think so. Just look at the calibre of my team," says Mr Glaston, hamming up a leer at Alice who starts giggling again.

"Calibre, that's a new name for it!"

"Yes. Thank you, Mr Jones."

In the film version of today, Lee Jones will be played by Lee Evans.

"What's our team strategy then, Sylvie?" Nigel asks.

"Let's come last so the others feel good," I suggest.

"Good plan, oh great leader," says Linda, saluting.

"Yeah, we could definitely do that with style."

I like the 'we' perhaps team building really does work.

The list of tasks declares we have to be photographed getting arrested, sitting on a lion in Trafalgar square and appearing on a West End stage. We manage all of those. OK, so we're not actually arrested but some very obliging policemen wave truncheons and handcuffs whilst they pose with Linda and me. It's more *Police Academy* than *Lethal Weapon.*

It's quite a scramble to get up on the plinth with the lions, but with Lee Evans-Jones pushing and Nigel pulling we manage. That certainly breaks the ice. You can't be aloof with someone who hauls you up to sit astride a bronze lion with them.

The assistant manager at The Dominion allows us to sit on the edge of the stage whilst he takes our picture. He doesn't ask us to send him a copy for Spotlight.

We answer several questions. For reference if you ever do this kind of thing, the height of the statue marking the start of the Great Fire is 202 feet. The numbers on the clock at Waterloo are red. You can't tell from a distance, but close up definitely bright red. Charlie Chaplin's statue is in Leicester Square.

We don't get to shake hands with the Prime Minister, or the Queen. None of us has a clue about the Crimean Memorial, or missing lamp posts on Tower Bridge. We spend more time admiring the sights than completing the quiz.

Nigel spots a post card of Prince Harry, which I buy and write, 'To Lovely Luscious Linda, lots of juicy kisses Harry HRH'. I just hope that's not treason.

When we all meet up again and compare results the group leaders give a team debrief. It's not until I'm back on the coach that I realise I actually stood up in front of everyone and spoke. Not just mumbled a few words but actually commented on our achievements.

"In our defence we had fun, stuck together as a team and achieved our stated mission of coming last."

I knew my team would laugh at my attempts at humour, I knew they'd yell agreement at my statement. These people are now my friends, especially Linda.

"I'm going to show my hubbie that postcard and let him draw his own conclusions. So that's my dream sorted. Looks like yours is next."

"Excuse me, Linda, would you mind exchanging places for a moment?" Mr Glaston sits next to me.

"I understand that you might be considering a permanent role in the company?"

"Oh yes, Mr Glaston, but I didn't think there was a vacancy at the moment."

"Strictly speaking there isn't yet. Alice, however, will be retiring in less than a year."

"But I couldn't possibly do her job; I'm still learning the computer system and, well..."

"It's alright," he interrupts. "We won't throw you in at the deep end. It is intended that very soon Linda will start shadowing Alice so she can take over when the time comes."

"Me... do Linda's job? She's so efficient and I'm still learning."

"Sylvie, you'll be thoroughly trained. As you say you are already learning. We don't expect perfection, just normal people, who have team spirit, are willing to work and hopefully have some fun too."

"That's me."

It is, not only does he believe it but, for the first time, so do I.

"One more thing, young Nigel wants to ask you something. It's up to you how you answer but please be gentle, he's awfully shy."

Everything goes into soft focus now, romantic music plays and the credits roll...

8. April Fool

"April, come and meet the new guy," her uncle Jerry called.

April smiled at the attractive mechanic. At least, she hoped he really was the new mechanic. Uncle Jerry was quite likely to be pulling her leg again. She didn't want to do another whole 'welcome to the company' speech and guided tour for a confused customer or a delivery driver who was too polite to interrupt.

"Hello," she said.

"Very pleased to meet you," Danny replied. He gave a heart-melting smile as he held out his hand.

His grip was gentle, but not weak. Those hands would be capable of tenderness as well as hard work.

"April does all the paperwork," Jerry said. "So you'll need to speak to her about your pay and all that sort of thing in a bit. I'll show you round and get you sorted with overalls first though."

"I'll see you later then, April," Danny said.

She was still gazing after him and wondering how long his politeness would last once he saw the example her uncle and the others set, when Uncle Jerry waved a hand in front of her eyes.

"Take it he meets with your approval, Dewdrop?"

"My name isn't Dewdrop and I'm sure he's a good worker or you wouldn't have employed him," she said in her most professional manner.

"Hmmm. Well, he can't work without tools. Order him a

set of left-handed spanners would you, Miss Raine?"

"Right, boss." Was he joking? She still could rarely tell. Rather than make a fool of herself with the suppliers yet again, she turned her attention to printing invoices. During the tea break she studied the other employees and realised they really were all right-handed expect for Danny.

When the break was over, Jerry ushered everyone back to work, leaving her and Danny alone. He gave her another lovely smile and then his tax forms and bank details.

"Thanks. I'll input all this on the system and give everything back before you leave tonight."

"Thank you."

"Is there anything else I can do for you?" she asked, trying not to sound too hopeful.

"Do you mind if I sit here for a minute and borrow your scissors to sort out these overalls?"

She looked him up and down and saw the ones he'd been given were far too long. She guessed he'd needed the bigger size because of his broad shoulders. "Of course not."

April did try to concentrate on her work as he removed the protective garment to reveal he was wearing only shorts and a sleeveless T-shirt underneath. She kept her gaze firmly averted from those muscular thighs and arms, tanned skin and the way that when he bent over his T-shirt rode up... Indeed she hardly noticed him at all. Even so, it wasn't long before she realised he was struggling to cut the bottoms off his overalls.

He saw her watching. "It's a bit awkward for me using right-handed scissors," he explained.

"Here, let me." She cut neatly through material and offered to pin them up.

For that he had to put the overalls back on, but as she had to kneel at his feet to work that was just as well.

"Thanks, that's a great help," he said when she'd finished. "I'll get some of that iron-on stuff to stop the ends from fraying."

She was so pleased at his gratitude and the fact he didn't expect her to sew them for him, just because she was a woman, that she volunteered to hem them. Of course the fact that he'd have to stay close by, barely clothed again whilst she stitched, had nothing to do with it.

"I really appreciate your help," he said. "If there's anything I can do to you, for you, I meant if there's anything I can do for you, just say." His face was very red as he backed out of the office.

As soon as he'd left her office she remembered something else she could do to help him and rang up to order his spanners. The loud wheezing on the line told her she'd been had again.

"That boss of yours is a card," the supplier said.

"His card is marked," April muttered.

She wasn't any happier the following week when one of the men got her to ask the owner of a classic car if the air in his spare tyre was in date.

April was fed up with not being taken seriously at work. Because she was the only girl employed at the garage the others treated her as though she was daft. It hadn't been so bad when she was still at school and did a bit of typing and filing for pocket money. Now she worked there full-time doing all the office work and accounts she deserved a little more respect.

She complained to her mum one evening, who said, "Jerry

does respect you, love. He wouldn't have given you a position of trust otherwise."

"He expects me to do all the menial stuff like make coffee for customers, saying it's because I'm the only one with clean hands."

"But you are, aren't you?"

That was true, but she was getting fed up with being the only one to take things seriously. Other than when her dad had died, Uncle Jerry treated his whole life as a joke and his staff took their lead from him. She acted as everyone's PA, reminding them to buy the gifts for their wives' birthdays and making sure they kept doctors' appointments. Meanwhile they called her Dewdrop and played silly tricks on her. She never used to mind, but Danny never used to work there.

One Friday, Uncle Jerry told her, "Young Danny really likes you, but he's too shy to say. As you're so keen to show you aren't just a typical girlie you should ask him out."

Like she'd fall for that! She'd been gullible enough to do stupid things such as go in search of a long stand when she'd started at the garage, but she was getting more wary lately.

When asked to order sparks for the angle grinder a while ago she'd seen through it straight away and she could see through this latest attempt to embarrass her. Danny would be embarrassed too of course if Uncle Jerry was right about him being shy.

April hoped that was the reason he barely spoke to her and it wasn't because Jerry had made up something about her. She was tempted to play a trick herself but wasn't willing to lower herself to Uncle Jerry's level. Besides, she'd probably mess it up. Instead she awarded herself an early finish and went shopping.

As soon as April arrived at work the following Monday, Uncle Jerry told her not to walk over the inspection pit that day.

"OK," she said. "Tea?"

"I'll make it if you like. My hands are clean for a change."

"It's OK, boss. I'll do it."

"Thanks, Dewdrop. You're a good kid."

April gave him a look.

"What I meant to say was, thank you, Miss Raine, you're an admirable employee."

"That's better. I'll let you have a chocolate biscuit for that."

She switched the kettle on and turned to start her computer. Propped against it was a note warning her not to walk across the inspection pit.

Danny was the next to arrive. His fingers brushed against hers as he accepted a mug of tea. Their gaze met, then he blushed and hurried out the office.

A minute later he was back. "There's something I have to say." He looked even more shy.

"Yes?"

"Jerry said to be sure you don't walk over the pit."

"Ah. Thanks."

As the other staff arrived two others urged her to avoid walking across the inspection pit. She hardly ever went out there, so why did they keep on about it? April almost asked, but sensed to do so would be to walk into a trap.

There was a call for Uncle Jerry from an important customer later that morning. April tried putting the call through to the workshop but got no reply. She looked out and saw him using a noisy piece of machinery on the other side of the pit. Although she waved he didn't look up.

"Sorry, he's dealing with something at the moment. Can I get him to call you back?"

"Can I wait? It's quite an urgent matter."

"Of course. I'll go and interrupt him."

As she crossed the workshop, April spotted cones were arranged strategically around the inspection pit. There were also three danger signs in front of it. Clearly someone wanted her to avoid walking across the strong wood which topped the pit and instead step on the tarpaulins which surrounded it.

They probably had glue or paint smeared on them, or something had been placed underneath to make a noise when she trod on it, or... It could be anything. April stepped onto the pit covering and fell straight through.

Uncle Jerry visited her in hospital, bringing Danny with him.

"Dewdrop, I'm so sorry," he said. He looked years older.

April knew that he'd carried her out of the pit himself. Although, since watching his brother die, he'd vowed never again to enter a hospital, he'd travelled with her in the ambulance and wouldn't leave the hospital until she'd come round. Mum told her he'd cried when told she needed an operation on her arm and had constantly blamed himself.

"It's OK, Uncle Jerry. Everyone did warn me and I'm going to be fine."

"But if it hadn't been for all my stupid jokes you'd have kept off the pit." His eyes glistened as though filling with tears.

April hated to see her uncle so unhappy. It wasn't like him

at all. Ever since she could remember he'd been the family joker, it was his way of showing affection. He made fun of her, but he'd also helped her pass her school exams and with so many other things. And of course he'd given her a good job. His jokes were part of his personality, a part she knew she'd miss if they stopped.

"It really wasn't your fault. Even as I fell I remembered you're always completely serious in the workshop, as a joke in there could be dangerous."

He stroked her cheek. "You're going to be OK? Really?"

"Really. Of course I won't be able to use the computer properly, while my arm is in plaster, as the mouse is on the right-hand side. I'll need help."

"I could do that, maybe," Danny tentatively suggested.

"You do that, lad." Uncle Jerry barely looked up from studying her medical chart.

April smiled. It hadn't occurred to him that left-handed Danny would have the same, completely fictitious, trouble. Even when Danny very gently held her hand to write on her cast Jerry didn't twig. She'd tell him, but not until after she'd had Danny's assistance and company for a day or two. Just about long enough for him to stop being so shy around her.

"We'll leave you in peace then, Dewdrop," Jerry said after a few minutes awkward conversation.

She smiled brightly to show she really was all right as they turned to wave from the end of the ward. April smiled even more widely when she saw Danny had written, 'please will you come out with me?' on her plaster cast.

The nurse's grin was broader still a few moments later when she stopped at the foot of April's bed.

"I think just this once I'm going to ignore doctor's orders."

"What do you mean?"

The nurse handed her the medical chart which sported a large sticky note saying, 'feed her nothing but cabbage soup and give her ice cold bed baths every hour.'

"What! Oooh, I'll get him." She looked at the words on her plaster cast. "And I'll have help."

9. It Started With A Kiss

I negotiated my way across the bar, back to my sister. The juke-box played, 'These Boots Are Made For Walking', which did nothing to improve my filthy mood. I tried to ignore the boys' laughter and avoid spilling my drink – unsuccessfully on both counts.

As usual for those days, I was angry. Angry at myself for causing the accident which left one leg needing scaffolding holding it together, and me up. I was angry at my own stubborn pride for insisting I carry the drinks after both my sister and the barman offered. And I was angry that as a result I looked like I'd already drunk more than I should, which amused the lads who should have been looking at me for my slim figure, long blonde hair and slinky top.

Most of all I was angry with Louise for the impossible request she'd just made of me.

"Darling, how are you!" a gorgeous stranger said. He bent his head to kiss me.

With my stupid leg and a wine glass in each hand, it was impossible to avoid being kissed, but even if strong legged and empty handed, I'd not have tried. I did mention he was gorgeous, right?

"Here, let me help." He took one glass and offered his arm for support.

I can't think what came over me, but instead of snapping at him for being patronising, I mumbled, "Thanks."

It wasn't because he recognised me; I knew he didn't. It wasn't because I realised he was trying to help, not imply I was helpless, because I didn't then see the good in people that way. Did I mention he was gorgeous?

"Hope they pay up," I bitched when we reached my sister.

He raised an eyebrow.

I pointed back to the boys, who were no longer laughing. "Your bet. 'Who'll kiss a cripple first', was it?"

"Yes, twenty quid I'll get. Not sure it was worth it, but hey." He shrugged, then flashed a dazzling smile at my sister. "Hi, I'm Martin."

She smiled back, sat upright and stuck her chest out in a way that reminded me we had similar taste in men.

"I'm Louise," she simpered as she shook his hand and forgot to let go. "Lucy's sister."

"We're twins," I said to avoid an all too predictable remark.

"You're not identical though, only one has a chip on her shoulder," Martin said.

Louise laughed.

I scowled.

Martin grinned.

"Hilarious," I said. "Now that everyone's amused themselves at my expense, will you please go away?"

"You were half right," he said. "We did have a bet that I'd kiss you, but it's me they were laughing at, not you."

"Really." I didn't even try to hide my cynicism.

"We noticed you both come in," Martin explained.

"You're only human," Louise said.

She had a point. Boys always looked at us, especially when we were together. I liked it – before the crash.

"It was obvious Louise here offered to help fetch the drinks and I said something about some people always making things difficult for themselves. The guys laughed, saying I was a fine one to talk. Blonde twins come into the bar and I'm not interested until it becomes obvious one of them has an attitude problem."

Louise said, "Sounds like you two were made for each other."

We did the laughing, scowling, grinning thing again. Then the music changed to a slow number.

"Want to dance, Lucy?" Martin asked.

I put more effort into the scowl.

"Sorry, I didn't hear you," Martin coaxed.

"Tell him, Lucy."

I turned the scowl on my traitorous sister, keeping my mouth shut so the rage couldn't leak out.

"Lucy has a bit of a limp," Louise said. "You might have noticed it?"

Martin nodded to admit the fact.

"It's permanent."

That time his nod suggested he'd guessed as much.

"So obviously her life is over," Louise continued. "She can't possibly attempt to get an interesting job, learn to drive or have a social life. Being my bridesmaid is absolutely out the question, even though we made a pact to do so when we were three years old."

I gasped. Not because she'd mentioned the thing we'd just quarrelled about, but because of the bitterness with which she'd spoken. I was hurt I wouldn't be her bridesmaid and she mine just as we'd always planned, but hadn't realised her emotion was disappointment for herself not pity for me.

Louise gulped down half a glass of wine and continued. "It's my big day and she says she's happy for me and wants everything to be perfect, but she can't bring herself to make a spectacle of herself walking down the aisle behind me, even though it would make me so happy to have her there supporting me."

Clearly she was more than just a little disappointed. Maybe she had a point. I'd accepted Martin's arm for support to walk across the pub. People had noticed, but it hadn't felt so bad.

"She can't dance with you, Martin. She might have to lean in close so as not to stumble."

Something told me that leaning close to Martin wouldn't feel at all bad.

"OK, I'll do it," I said.

"Walk down the aisle?" Martin asked.

"Let's just start with a dance and take it from there, shall we?" I said.

It was a feeble attempt at a joke, but Martin laughed.

Louise laughed.

I laughed.

Then Martin and I danced. We danced badly. As Louise had hinted, I did need to lean on Martin, but he didn't seem to mind.

Right then I decided it was time I stopped minding so much about my limp. True my last boyfriend had jilted me at the hospital bedside, but we'd been arguing long before the accident. Perhaps he'd told the truth when he said it wasn't because of my leg.

I did walk down the aisle at my sister's wedding. The guests thought it was so cute the way I rested one hand on a pageboy's shoulder and held the flower girl's hand with the other. That help wasn't needed going back out as Martin was there to support me.

He seems to want the job permanently. I haven't yet made my mind up about that, but I will always be grateful for that first kiss which taught me that standing on my own two feet wasn't something I had to do without help.

10. The Copier

"The photocopier has broken down again, Angela," the office manager moans.

"Never mind, if you've got anything that needs doing I'll take it over to accounts."

"You're a star, you never complain about having to trudge over there."

I like to use the copier in the accounts department. It's in a narrow corridor. People have difficulty walking past without making physical contact. Peter Langdon doesn't have that problem. He doesn't make any attempt to stop his thigh brushing against my hip. If I happen to be bent over, programming the machine or filling the staples, he'll get up real close and reach over me, pressing all the right buttons. I often happen to be bending over as he passes.

I really should take control of myself. I'm a mother of three and today is my fifteenth wedding anniversary. Our marriage is happy enough, and I love the kids, but it's all become a dull routine. Mornings are a mad scramble to get everyone fed, dressed and to work or school on time. The evenings are pretty much the same only in reverse. The weekends are taken up with the children's sports, housework, mowing the lawn.

Then there is work. I returned only six months ago, and very quickly it was as if I'd never left. The computers are more modern and there are new faces, but I soon settled in. The work is familiar, so is the office banter, the rivalries and romances. At work I am Angela again, not just a wife and mother.

I met my husband here. We started on the same day, soon spending every lunch break together. Rumours of our engagement were the talk of the company. I overheard it being discussed in the toilets three days before he actually proposed! That was a long time ago. His post is now filled by a pretty red-head. There are plenty of rumours about her, but they don't interest me.

The day I returned to work was Peter Langdon's first day as head of accounts. We had lunch together in the canteen. We do that almost every day now, although occasionally we go out to a pub. I know that people have started to talk, but let them, I'm not doing anything wrong. The man is gorgeous and his flirting makes me feel like a girl again, but it's just harmless fun.

"Perhaps we could have a drink together, after work one evening?" Peter had suggested.

It sounded innocent enough. My children all had after school activities on Thursdays. Just one white wine spritzer, where was the harm? His hand brushed mine as we'd reached together for our drinks. He had sat close, his lips almost touching my ear in order to be heard over the noise. That first Thursday evening drink has now become a regular occurrence.

I think about my forthcoming wedding anniversary. The first one had been wonderful. My husband arranged for us to take the afternoon off work. He took me to lunch at The Belvedere, and we spent the rest of the weekend in the hotel. By the second anniversary, I was heavily pregnant. There were no more romantic afternoons off. One year I was actually in labour. Since then it's been an exchange of cards, flowers for me and I cook him his favourite meal. That will happen in a few hours, but first there's lunch with Peter.

"I thought we'd try somewhere different for lunch today, The Belvedere."

I almost say something then, as I remember that first anniversary. I nod; this time it is just lunch on offer. On the drive there I reason with myself, being a wife and mother surely doesn't mean I'm not entitled to any fun?

Peter leads me across the lobby, "I think the restaurant is that way," I say.

"You're right, but room service is this way."

He leads me upstairs.

There is champagne on ice, but he doesn't open it. He places an arm around my waist, pulling me close. He strokes my cheek, then brushes my lips with the gentlest of kisses. I don't move. I admit to myself that I'd known this would happen, I just didn't know when.

"Don't worry about work, they're not expecting us back," he tells me.

"What did...?"

"Don't worry about anything," he whispers, running his fingers down my spine. I moan softly and lean my body against him.

Perhaps we shouldn't be doing this? He kisses me again and it is already too late, I can't resist him.

His hand strokes my back as he nuzzles my neck, whispering endearments. He is so gentle, so controlled. I can stand it no longer, and undo his tie. I try to pull off his jacket, but I'm too impatient and just tangle up his arms. He laughs and steps a little away from me. Alternately, we remove clothing from each other, kissing and nibbling every inch of freshly exposed skin as we do so.

Later we lie entwined in the huge bed. He kisses me again, before sliding out of bed. He opens his briefcase and hands me an envelope, "Happy anniversary, Mrs Langdon."

"Why thank you, Mr Langdon. Your card is at home, but if you come here I'll give you something else," I suggest.

An hour and a half later, although we are slightly dishevelled, we just manage to pick our children up from school on time.

11. Let's Pretend

"Welcome to Tenerife, Amanda. I'm your Fantasy-Sun rep for this holiday. Please make your way to coach three. It won't be long to wait, there's just one more person to come."

Amanda is tired; she'd woken at just after five. Travelling first by bus from home, then ferry from Gosport to Portsmouth, then trains, a plane and apparently now an automobile. If there are other forms of transport, Amanda doesn't want to experience them.

The coach driver waves at her, gesturing enquiringly at his coach. When she nods he strides towards her and takes her cases, which he squeezes into the luggage compartment. He hands Amanda a plastic beaker and holds up a glass jug. She can see condensation beading on its surface and slices of lime and strawberries floating in the clear, golden liquid. She nods eagerly. The cup is quickly filled. It's emptied even more rapidly.

"Thank you," she whispers with genuine gratitude.

Her cup is refilled as the rep arrives with the last holidaymaker. Amanda climbs onto the air conditioned coach. She sips her drink as the rather attractive latecomer sits next to her. For the first time since booking, this holiday seems like it might actually be a good idea. Two weeks away from drizzly English weather, who wouldn't enjoy that?

"Can I have some more of that juice, love?" someone asks the rep after welcome packs have been handed out.

"You can, but it's not juice love, more like love juice."

Cheers and wolf whistles fill the coach.

"Actually it's sangria," the rep explains.

"Thought that was red?"

"Ordinary sangria is. You're drinking champagne sangria. Nothing but the best for Fantasy-Sun's guests."

The jug is refilled from a large plastic barrel and passed round.

"Pure fantasy, that's what this holiday is about. Fantasy Beach, your resort, is built on re-claimed land. It's all make believe. You've all come here to enjoy yourselves right?"

There is a half-hearted response.

"No more sangria till you lot wake up a bit."

The groans and appeals this threat provokes are a lot more convincing.

"I'll try again. Have you come to have fun?"

"Yes!" everyone yells, including Amanda, to her surprise.

"You want to escape your boring everyday lives and live a fantasy for a couple of weeks?"

"Yes!"

"And forget your boring everyday selves and be the person you always wanted to for a fortnight?"

"Yes!"

Amanda yells loudest of all. She wants to stop being 'good old reliable, can't get a boyfriend but will babysit or work extra shifts at the drop of a hat because she's got no life of her own' Amanda. She doesn't want to be pale, freckly with chunky thighs. She doesn't want mousey hair that never goes straight. She wants to be interesting and sought after for her wit, charm and looks. Here she will not be the settled for option because she is always available. Here she will display some spirit.

The holiday rep outlines the programme of events and encourages everyone to develop a new persona. They can be anything they like. It isn't lying, just a bit of fun. Everyone will join in, knowing it's all just a game.

Amanda thinks of the long floaty clothes she packed to avoid sunburn and hide her less attractive features. Mostly they are neck to ankle, long-sleeved kaftans. She remembers too her habit of day dreaming that unkind people suggest makes her look slightly stupid. Amanda Smith re-invents herself as Siobhan Desire the poet.

"G'day, mate." The man sitting beside her offers his hand.

Taking it, she looks into his smiling eyes and decides some of her poems are going to be rather romantic.

"Hello, I'm Siobhan. I'm a poet. You look like a surfer. I assume you are one of our Antipodean cousins."

"Eh?"

"Your accent, I thought it was Australian?"

"Yeah that's right. Aussie surfer dude, that's me. Name's Dillon. What sort of poems do you write then?"

"Very deep and meaningful ones," Amanda gently squeezes his hand. "Perhaps I could read some to you, one moonlit night?"

"Yeah after a barbie, that'd be great, Sheila."

"Siobhan."

"Yeah I know, I was just being Aussie."

They both grin at the misunderstanding. Dillon looks down at their still clasped hands. "This is going to be a lot of fun. I hope I can keep it up for the whole holiday."

"Hey, someone's in for a treat, guy in front reckons he can

keep it up for a fortnight," is yelled down the coach.

After this everyone begins to introduce themselves. There is a gynaecologist, an RAF pilot, pole dancer, dental nurse, two actresses and a train spotter who hopes it won't be too hot for him to wear his anorak. Melanie the pole dancer claims they'll all be hot when she wears her outfit. She holds up some sequins, held together with thin straps of elastic. In the real world they'd be hairbands, but with a bit of imagination they do look rather like part of a skimpy costume.

"You won't be that's for sure," says the man sitting opposite.

"Yes I will, I'm very energetic."

Amanda guesses that Melanie is going to be very popular.

Dillon makes a point of spending time with Amanda. Whilst they're sunbathing he tells her that his oil-well owning, millionaire father sent him on this holiday to avoid the stress of waiting for his degree results. She guesses the father is part of the fantasy and asks him why a surfer chose this resort rather than one famous for its waves.

"Muscle strain. Want to administer first aid?" he says offering the suntan lotion.

That'll teach her for trying to get closer to the real man.

Amanda finds it easy to maintain her image. All that's needed is for her to carry a notebook and occasionally ask people if they can think of a word that rhymes with frangipani.

On a trip to a liqueur factory they enter a room filled with lemons.

"Smells like sunlight," she says, meaning the washing-up

liquid, but not explaining when she realises how poetic the phrase sounds.

The holiday really boosts her confidence. Knowing she's unlikely to meet any of them again, Amanda chats, jokes and flirts. People respond, laughing at her jokes and wanting her company. She's not as popular as Melanie and her insecure sequins, but she's liked by everyone. She doesn't want to stop being happy and go back to being the miserable timid girl she was before.

Amanda has great fun with Dillon. Neither of them is keen on the loud smoky disco, so they spend their evenings strolling along the beach. They watch the palm trees become silhouettes against the sunset, then relax together on beach towels. In the tropically warm and dark nights, she is far less self-conscious and inhibited than ever before. With Dillon there is no need for embarrassment.

Amanda confesses that she booked the holiday to cheer herself up after a broken relationship.

"You're better off without him. He didn't deserve you. You were right to dump him."

"Actually he dumped me, but you're right; I am better off without him. He only asked me out because he's so irritating most other girls can't put up with him."

"So why did you?"

"I thought I wouldn't get another boyfriend, that he was better than nothing. Stupid eh?"

"Yes. Don't underestimate yourself. Hey, two weeks of fantasy and I chose to spend it with you."

"You really like me?"

"You are funny, intelligent, kind, and blonde. What more could a guy want?"

It's true, her unruly mousey hair is now a sun-kissed blonde mop of curls. She's fun to be with because she's relaxed and enjoying herself. Her personality and intelligence show now, rather than being hidden behind her nerves.

"I thought you were just being friendly because you sat next to me on the bus and I was on my own."

"Trust me, Siobhan, blokes aren't like that." He kisses her gently then takes her hand and pulls her back towards the hotel complex.

"Come on, Sheila, let's go and grab a couple of tinnies and make the most of our time together."

She realises then that he'd not sounded Australian when he said he enjoyed being with her. All the nice things he'd said were real, he meant them.

Dillon sits next to her on the bus back to the airport.

"So what happens now, Sheila?"

"What do you mean?"

"When do we go back to being ourselves?"

"I'm not sure I want to go back," Amanda says.

"Me neither really, perhaps we don't have to."

"We can't live a fantasy forever. That would never work."

"Can't we stay in touch? We don't need to lose out on the fun we've been having."

"I flew from Gatwick and you travelled from Liverpool, so we can't expect to meet often. I thought this was just a sort of holiday romance. You did kind of hint that."

"You're right, but we could still be friends," Dillon suggests.

"Really?"

"Course we can, Sheila. We could phone, or email. We can remind each other that we're fun popular people who someone else chose to spend their entire holiday with."

"That would be great. But you don't need the fantasy. You'll get your degree and a great job and impress all the girls with your surfing on all the holidays you'll have to take to avoid executive stress."

"No degree. I'm a bank clerk. I can't surf, I can barely swim. You are the one who doesn't need any fantasies. I guess you're not a professional poet though. It's not really something many people make a living from."

"I'm not a poet at all. My name is Amanda, I'm really shy and boring. The whole thing was a fake."

"Amanda is a much better name. I was dreading having to type Siobhan on those emails. I haven't a clue how it's spelt."

"I have, but only because it's my aunt's name."

On the flight back Amanda remembers that shy or not she had spoken to Dillon first and had made him her friend. She smiles at the girl sitting next to her.

"Did you have a nice holiday?" Amanda asks.

"Oh fantastic. I met a racing driver. He's gorgeous and rich and crazy about me. He's going to come and see me when he gets back from Monaco."

"He sounds nice." Amanda is aware her tone is doubtful.

"Did you meet anyone then?"

"An Australian son of an oil millionaire. He's a surfer?" She deliberately phrases this to show she doubts the truth of her words.

"Can he swim?"

"No."

"I don't think Pablo can drive."

They giggle helplessly. The rest of the flight is taken up with drinking wine, eating peanuts and comparing notes on their holiday loves.

"Oh, Amanda. If only the holiday fantasy could go on forever."

"Well, Emily, mine's going to. I'm fed up with being a shy doormat. I'm going to find myself a proper job – I'm a part-time waitress at the moment. I'm going to have my hair highlighted when the sun bleached bits grow out. I'm going to be a fun person."

"Way to go! I don't suppose you live near Portsmouth? You sound like someone I want to be friends with."

They're delighted to discover they live on the same bus route.

The day after her return Amanda receives an email from Dillon.

'Hi, Amanda-Sheila. Remember you are a great girl!! Live the dream!! Luv Dave-Dillon the Dude.'

She replies. 'You're so right, I'm far too good for a surfer dude like you. I'm going to go to creative writing classes with my new best friend Emily. I'll become a poet. She's going to be an author. We'll live happily ever after with a couple of nice, charming bank managers.'

It's not long before she gets a response.

'Hmm. I'll think I'd better apply for the management training course. I didn't think I was bright enough, but since I met you I've become more confident. Luv Dave.

PS Apparently there are trains between Liverpool and Portsmouth.'

12. Lame Ducks

I missed her when she stopped coming. Not surprising really as she used to make a special effort to throw a few pieces of food my way. Suppose she'd seen me on land and knew about my leg. It wasn't just self-interest though. I missed her because of the effect on him. Sometimes it seems humans experience the same emotions as us ducks.

He used to walk past the lake most days. Calling it walking is being generous really. He dragged himself round. Couldn't tell why. He was old, but I've seen much older humans who don't walk as though they're carrying the troubles of the whole flock.

He passed her a couple of times as she threw corn for us. He walked better those days than when their visits to the park didn't coincide. Then one time he stopped to watch and his face did that crinkling thing they do. Not the one that happens right after one of their chicks drops an ice cream and just before they scream. This was the other kind, like the chicks do when they see us crowding round for a feed.

The next time he passed her, he stopped quite near and threw a crust of bread into the water. They nodded at each other and crinkled. After that they always came at the same time each day. They arrived from different sides of the park, met at the lake, threw food together and talked. I rarely heard what about. The other ducks squawked, blocking out the sound unless I got really close. I guess part of it was what to feed ducks as he soon stopped bringing bread and switched to the more nutritious seeds, corn and rice which she brought. I got fond of those two and hoped come spring they'd build a nest together.

At first it seemed they would. As it got colder they stood closer together. When ice formed on the edge of the lake he held her arm as she reached out to ensure some food reached me. Then she stopped coming.

I hadn't noticed how much better his walking was until I watched it deteriorate, day by day. He spent a long time throwing the food and kept looking around him. His throws got shorter and shorter, often barely reaching the water. That meant I had no chance of getting any.

One day he just stood at the lakeside with the bag of food in his hand. Soon the other ducks gave up and went in search of more promising humans, but I stayed. I don't think he saw anything at all as he stared at the water. I paddled to the edge hoping to attract his attention and remind him to throw. When that didn't work I scrambled out and took a few steps towards him.

"The little lame duck," he whispered before tipping peas out at my feet. I quickly ate what I could before the others arrived. He walked away, more slowly than ever.

The next few days he waited until I was the only duck about and gave me the lot. Then one day another female arrived. She was much younger. He seemed surprised when she spoke. Without any other ducks around I heard most of what they said. 'Broken' was bad I knew as the chicks do the crinkling and screaming routine if told a toy is broken. 'Hip' and 'visiting' I couldn't even guess at though I learned one new human word; nurse. That's what young female humans are called.

He dropped the peas at my feet again but when I glanced up after a couple of beakfulls he was still there. His face was crinkled but I couldn't tell which kind of crinkling it was. When he left he moved easily. Maybe he was going to nest with the nurse?

Every day for quite a while he came and threw food, taking care I got some. He was always alone though. Then one day he arrived late and from the side of the park where she used to come from. The older female I mean, not the nurse. He was still alone though. He threw feed just as before, except there was more of it. That became his routine until the day he arrived later still and with her. I was pleased to see her even though she wasn't carrying anything.

She took only little steps and held his arm for support the whole way, even when they stopped for him to feed us.

They come together every day now so they must be nesting. I'm delighted and not just because they've added grapes to my rations.

13. Bowled Over

Molly had known she wouldn't enjoy the bowls club's annual BBQ and trophy presentation evening and was therefore proved right. Several people approached her and Tim, wanting to chat. Molly didn't encourage them. She knew the moment they got into conversation they'd start talking about bowls and she'd be excluded.

She didn't eat any of the profiteroles decorated with red and blue icing spots to represent bowls.

"It's silly, why's everything got to be about bowls?" she asked Tim.

"Because it's a bowls club, lass. Anyway it's just a bit of fun, they still taste the same."

Molly picked at her food between large gulps from her gin and tonic. "Can you get me another one of these, and make sure they use a fresh bottle of tonic, I don't want some that's going flat."

"You don't look very happy, love," Tim told his wife when he returned from the bar.

"I don't know anyone; I don't understand half of what people are talking about, especially the speeches. I don't know why I'm here," Molly replied.

"I thought you wanted to come."

"What on earth gave you that idea?"

"You said that since I'd retired, I've spent all my time at the club, that you think we're drifting apart and you want us to spend more time together."

"This wasn't what I had in mind."

"What was then?"

Molly was saved from replying by the club president's announcement that he was about to present the Herbert Shield.

"This prestigious award," he informed them, "is an annual award presented to the club member with the highest aggregate score in all the competition matches. Great dedication is needed to win it."

"I can't believe I've got to sit through all of this when you didn't even win anything," Molly complained.

The moment she'd said it she wished she hadn't. Tim had really hoped to win this year. His skill at the game had improved greatly since retirement had provided more practice time. His rivalry with his friend Bert had increased too. More than once Tim had boasted that this year Bert would be applauding his success. Tactfully, Bert hadn't reminded him of that when the scores were added up. He hadn't mentioned it when Molly and Tim arrived this evening either. He'd just slapped his friend on the back, tried to welcome Molly and compliment her on her dress. He had saved them seats, but Molly had refused to sit at his table. She soon regretted that. It wasn't right to punish him for her unhappiness.

Molly tried to concentrate on the president's speech.

"To be in with a chance of winning you need to play in almost every match, both home and away. Not just individually either, scores in doubles and team events count too. It is unusual to have an award that counts your team score, but Iain Herbert who instigated the award was a visionary. When he became chairman of the club..."

The chairman went on and on and on about the things that

Iain Herbert, and his wife too it seemed, had done to build the club up from almost nothing to whatever it was now. Molly couldn't imagine why he'd bothered and wished he hadn't.

"The club can be justly proud that it now has four teams, two top class men's teams, a marvellous ladies team and one for improvers to gain experience."

Molly shuffled in her seat. "Why doesn't he get on with it? I bet he goes through all this every year."

"The club has won the County Cup for the last consecutive three years and has twice reached the regional finals," the president continued. "Without further ado, I'd like to announce that this year's winner is Bert Bloomfield."

Tim clapped vigorously and congratulated his friend as he made his way to collect the trophy. Molly clapped too; she didn't want Bert to think her earlier rudeness had been sour grapes because he'd beaten Tim. She felt proud of her husband. She knew he was bitterly disappointed not to be the winner himself. She also knew that only two points separated the men.

The following day Tim said, "As we went to the bowls club yesterday, we'll do whatever you like today."

Molly felt bad again. Tim, except when he was at the bowls club, was always ready to do whatever Molly wanted. The trouble was that Molly didn't have a hobby herself.

"There's a sale on in that fancy department store in town, you won't want to go there though. You don't like shopping."

"McKenzie's? I don't mind, if that's what you want to do. We could have tea and a cake in the restaurant."

"Oooh, I don't know, Tim. It's a bit posh..."

"It's not too posh for you, Molly; you're a proper lady

anyone can see that and I can always hide behind you."

Molly squeezed his hand, not only was he taking her shopping, which he hated, but he was actually trying to pretend that it would be fun. She should have tried harder at the bowls club.

She enjoyed looking at all the fancy things in the shop.

"Will you just look at the price of that?" she said as she picked up a jar of preserved cherries. "D'you think people really use these?" as she showed him an olive stoner.

Tim joined in the game; he tried on some hats and then sat on chairs in the furniture department.

Even after the special discounts, most of the items were too expensive to tempt Molly. After two hours, all she had bought were some new pillows. Tim carried them, often lagging behind his wife as they were not easy to manoeuvre between the bargain hunting customers and the artfully displayed, breakable goods.

"Just one more department, and then I think we'll be ready for that tea," Molly declared.

"And the cake."

Molly nodded her agreement. They had reached the sportswear section.

"You taking up a sport or summat, Molly lass?"

"Me? Don't be daft. No, I thought you could do with a new set of bowling whites."

They found some that fitted perfectly. They weren't much reduced in price, but Molly decided they were of good enough quality to be worth the money.

Tim, carrying the new pillows and now the large bag of clothing, lagged behind Molly as she edged through the crowds towards the ladies wear department. She'd lost sight of him completely when she heard a cry followed by people shouting. Although aware that something had happened, she couldn't see what the fuss was about. She couldn't find Tim to ask him. Members of staff hurried to the area and began encouraging people to move on. She heard mention of an ambulance as she wandered around looking for her husband.

Molly had just decided that Tim must have been ushered by staff into another department, when she heard her name mentioned on the shop's public address system.

"Would Molly Harris please make herself known to a member of staff."

Daft beggar has gone and got himself lost, she thought. She couldn't be annoyed though, she felt quite important to hear her name announced like that. It made her feel that she had a right to be there.

"That's me, I'm Molly Harris," she told the first person she found dressed in McKenzie's uniform.

"Please come with me," the woman said.

She didn't look very happy. Molly hoped her and Tim wouldn't be in trouble for causing a fuss.

"This is Mrs Harris," her escort told a man in a suit, who was obviously important.

"Mrs Harris, please come with me."

Molly followed, feeling quite nervous now. He led her back to where she'd lost sight of Tim.

"Where's Tim?" she asked.

She didn't need a reply, she could see him on the floor. He wasn't moving. Why didn't the silly fool get up? Shop staff where around him, one of her new pillows was under his head.

The staff moved aside and urged her to Tim's side. That's

when she saw how pale he was. She didn't think he was dead. They'd have covered him up surely, if he was? The shop lights seemed to fail and her legs stopped holding her up. Molly felt someone's arm support her. A chair was pushed in place for her to sink onto.

"The ambulance is on its way," the important looking man told her.

Molly went to hospital in the ambulance too. She learnt that Tim had slipped, landed awkwardly and broken his ankle. He could hardly speak to her, his face was a horrible grey colour and all sweaty, even his eyes looked wrong. Molly tried to smile and tell him he was fine, but she knew she wasn't fooling anyone.

A doctor soon examined Tim and arranged for X-rays.

"Your husband has had a nasty injury, he will need to stay in hospital for a while, but I'm confident he will, in time, make a good recovery."

Someone at the hospital made arrangements for Molly to be taken home and took details of Tim's car that was still in McKenzie's car park.

The following day the department store's delivery van arrived. The items Molly had bought and forgotten about were carried to her front door, as well as a hamper of food. She was assured that the car could be left until someone was able to collect it. There would, of course, be no parking charges.

Molly began to look through the hamper. She found a jar of preserved cherries, just like the one she'd picked at earlier.

"Tim, will you look..."

Molly began to cry. With tears in her eyes she unfolded Tim's new bowling whites. She removed the tags and vowed never again to complain about his bowls, just as long as he recovered enough to continue playing.

The next day, Molly was at the hospital, ready and waiting the very minute visiting hours began. Tim was sat up in bed, his cheeks were pink and he smiled at her.

"Look at them, lass; you ever see the like?"

He gestured to the floral display on his locker. Molly didn't recognise any of the green and red flowers, she couldn't place the peculiar looking leaves and had no idea from what plant the contorted twigs were gathered. The whole thing was wrapped in cellophane, tastefully marked with the McKenzie's logo.

Molly sat on the hard chair by Tim's bed and held his hand as he explained about the treatment he had received and what was to follow. He would be fine again eventually, but it would take time.

"I still don't really know what happened," Molly said. "Did you fall over something?"

"No, lass, there wasn't anything there. I just lost my footing, don't know why."

Tim was worried about letting Bert down in a forthcoming match.

"Don't worry, love. I'll tell him and he'll understand."

At home, she realised that because she'd distanced herself from Tim's hobby she didn't know Bert's phone number and couldn't look it up because she couldn't remember his surname. She couldn't ring the club because she had no idea who she should speak to. She would have to visit the club house. Luckily, someone recognised her as she walked from the car park. They were very kind to her.

Molly soon realised what good friends her husband's clubmates were. Tim had a constant stream of visitors and Molly received frequent calls, offering any help that might be needed. Several members of the ladies team called, offering company. She realised that they didn't care if she was interested in bowls or not, they just wanted to offer support. It was Molly who'd pushed them away, not the other way round.

She missed Tim. When he'd been working, Molly had known nothing about his job. She'd shunned his colleagues fearing they'd talk nothing but shop and exclude her. Now she took no interest in his hobby. It wasn't Tim or his job or the bowls club that was the problem, it was Molly herself. It wasn't too late for her to change.

Of course, Tim couldn't play bowls for a while after he left hospital. He could still watch though, take an interest and cheer on his friends. So could Molly. She drove him to every match, even the away ones.

Tim didn't win the Herbert Shield that year either; he'd missed too many games. Neither did Bert; without Tim his doubles score wasn't good enough. Tim won it the following year, beating Bert by two clear points. Molly was so proud of him she couldn't speak. Instead, she handed him a slice of the cake she'd made. It was iced in green and decorated with marzipan bowls, players and score board.

As she polished his shield Molly realised she was the real winner.

14. The Domino Effect

"Lucie, do you know about dominoes?" Matias asked me during our coffee break.

I'd been taught to play by my grandparents. When Granny was young and boys asked her out her father would invite them to the pub for a game of dominoes. How they played determined whether or not he'd let Granny go out with them. He'd check if they cheated, weren't sensible enough to learn, let him win to suck up or were ungracious in victory. Only Grandad had passed the test.

The story had always struck me as romantic and I'd believed dominoes would lead me to my true love. Blushing slightly at that thought, I started to explain about the game.

I was interrupted by one of my colleagues.

"If you've got time to sit about chatting I assume you've finished the West Springs report?"

"Nearly. I'll have it for you Wednesday, no problem."

"Wednesday! That's when I have to present it to the client. Don't think I don't know you're trying to sabotage my chances of getting on the exchange placement. I told you I needed it today at the latest."

"No, Sally, you didn't."

"You're getting as bad as him," she stabbed a finger towards Matias. "Always pretending not to understand so you don't have to do any work. You'd better go and explain to Mr Sanchez."

She was being unfair, but if I ran to the boss to say so I'd just get her in trouble. We'd both be better off if I worked through lunch to finish the report and kept quiet.

"I am sorry, Lucie. Have I caused you a problem?"

"It's not your fault, Matias. Now about dominoes... To decide who goes first each player draws a tile and adds up how many dots, which are called pips, are on it..." I stopped when I saw him frown. He obviously wasn't following me. Matias moved here from Chile eight months ago and there are a few things he just doesn't get. It's usually me he asks as the others at work laugh at him or pretend they can't understand.

"Don't you realise it just makes you look stupid?" I'd asked them. Matias has quite a strong accent, but his English is good and he makes perfect sense if anyone takes the trouble to listen.

The others demonstrated their intelligence and maturity by chanting, "Lucie fancies Matty, Lucie fancies Matty". They couldn't be bothered to get his name right, but it was obvious who they meant. I'd overreacted a bit, mostly because they were right.

Matias is attractive and pleasant company, but he's only here for a year, most of which has gone, so wasn't looking for a long-term relationship and I wasn't looking to get my heart broken with a short term fling. That didn't mean we couldn't be friends and help each other out. Matias was helping me with my Spanish during our breaks. You can't beat learning from a native speaker, especially when he's as patient as Matias.

The company has interests in several Spanish speaking companies and we sometimes deal with them by phone. Although they always communicate in English I thought it would be polite to exchange a few words in their own language.

Thinking something had got lost in translation, I drew a domino tile on my notepad. "Are we talking about the same thing?"

Matias leant across me and drew another. His was a one and two, mine a double five.

"I'd go first," I said.

"If you're hoping to sleep your way to the top you're going after the wrong man," Lou sneered in my ear.

I don't think Matias heard, or he might have said something about the way she'd come on to him when he first arrived. Mr Sanchez had explained that when Matias returned to Chile, someone from our branch would have the chance to accompany him. Lou lost all interest in Matias after he told us it wasn't him who'd be making the selection.

"Mr Sanchez wants to see you. You're late for your performance review," she continued.

"Mine isn't until this afternoon."

"It was changed. You must have seen my note?"

I hadn't and didn't entirely believe she'd written one.

"That exchange placement is as good as mine." Lou sashayed away.

Mr Sanchez asked about my flexibility and whether I was the sort to 'go the extra mile'. As I'm always keen to try new things and pride myself on doing a good job I said yes, but the sparkle in his eye combined with what Lou had said left me worried I might have given the wrong impression and I started blathering on about my typing speed and the training courses I'd like to enrol for. I get flustered like that quite often, so have no chance of being selected for the placement.

I worked on the report for Sally until Matias waved a

leaflet from a pizza delivery company.

"Domino,s pizza. Did I say it wrong?"

"No. No you didn't. The mistake was mine." I pointed out the design on the box which represents the playing pieces.

"They have an offer on and I thought maybe we could share a meal this evening?"

"I, oh, I..."

He'd made such suggestions before and I'd always turned him down. Each time it got harder to do.

"Lucie, can I have a word?" Mr Sanchez asked, rescuing me from my predicament.

"It's about that extra mile, or rather seven and a half thousand of them."

"But... I'd checked how far away Matias would be from me when he returned home and that was the same distance.

Mr Sanchez confirmed he was offering me the placement. "I see you're surprised. Think about it and let me know, eh?"

Not trusting myself to speak coherently I nodded, then went in search of Matias.

After thin crust pepperoni that evening, I tipped the old black and white tiles out of the box and taught Matias to play. I got flustered again explaining the rules because our hands touched as we reached for tiles and our gaze met whenever I glanced at him. That didn't bother Mathis; he was a fast learner. After the first two games he beat me fair and square every time.

"Beginner's luck?" he suggested.

I knew different, just as I knew Great-grandad would have approved of Matias.

15. Lizzie's Last Stand

As I listen to the almost inhuman cries of my captors, I try to keep control of my breathing. Breath in, hold it, breath out. Deep regular breaths, that's the secret. I don't want to risk having an asthma attack; my inhaler is in my handbag and I didn't have a chance to pick it up when they grabbed me. They might take pity on me if I started wheezing, but I don't want to put that to the test.

The first thing they did was to put on a blindfold, so I'm not even sure exactly where I am. Trying to remember details gives me something to concentrate on. People knew where I was going; they'll eventually notice I'm missing.

I think through what's happened and concentrate on all that's going on around me, hoping for clues. The few words I overhear aren't much help. There's something about heading for a ridge and mention of horses; we could be anywhere. They seem to be disguising their voices, but they sound young. They're using what I guess are gang names. Little Dog, I think one of them was called and I know there's a clear leader as the others refer to him as The Chief.

I hardly struggle as they tie me to a chair; if they think I'm cooperating they might not bind me so tightly. Perhaps they think they have me beat, as thankfully they don't gag me before they leave.

Once I hear their voices fade into the distance, I begin trying to release myself. Thanks to a tomboy childhood spent playing games with my brothers, I'm no stranger to being tied up and I'd managed to take a few precautions. I'd hooked a finger around my jacket sleeve and yanked it down as my arms were pulled behind me. I also crossed my wrists as they were bound. Bringing them into line now and wiggling the sleeve away creates just enough slack for me to work my hands free. The blindfold is simply a scarf wound round my face and easily pulled off.

My legs are tightly lashed to the chair legs, fortunately I'm wearing my cowboy boots today. It's slow and fiddly work, but I manage to inch down the zips and slip my feet out. Without my feet in them it's easy to untangle them from the bindings.

I put them back on and walk carefully and quietly to the door. It's locked; of course it is. As I rattle the handle in irritation, I hear a sound from behind me. I am not alone.

I freeze, I hadn't expected that. Is this a fellow captive, or a member of the group who've lured me here? I turn to face him as confidently as I can.

It's Dave.

As though I'm in a dream where even the most bizarre events seem perfectly reasonable, I don't even wonder why he's there. It almost makes sense that, if I've been captured, bound and gagged by some bunch of youths, Dave will be there to witness it.

It's not much consolation to note that, if anything, he's in a worse predicament than I am. His hands and feet are still tied and there is sticking tape over his mouth. I can't blame the gang for that, there have been times when I'd have liked to slap tape over his mouth myself.

"They got you too then?" I ask.

He nods.

Oh Lizzie, I chastise myself, what a dumb question; of

course they got him. He hardly tied himself up and stuck tape over his own mouth. No wonder the man thinks you're an idiot. Not that I care what he thinks, I hastily remind myself. He's a male chauvinist pig.

It's true my heart beats a little faster whenever I meet him, but that's just because he annoys me so much. It has nothing to do with him being six feet tall, having perfect white teeth and blue eyes that crinkle at the corners whenever he's amused. Especially as that amusement is generally at my expense.

Despite everything, I can't help smiling as I remember our previous meetings and how, at the time, I'd thought things couldn't get any worse. I'd heard so much about him from his sister, my best friend Sheila, that I'd rather been looking forward to meeting him. She'd made him sound wonderful, and at first glance she was right. He's got the looks and charming smile. He's even got the deep sexy voice. Normally that would make me go weak at the knees, but not when I hear what he has to say.

Suddenly, I realise something amazing. The man who thinks girls should stick to the kitchen is now bound and gagged waiting for me to rescue him. The situation is just too tempting, I can't help taking advantage.

"I take it you're not about to rescue me then?" I ask.

He mumbles from behind the tape.

"I'd love to untie you, but I might chip a nail," I taunt in my best girlie simper.

If I didn't know better, I'd think he was laughing, it must just be anger making his eyes shine. I know it's not kind, but I can't help reminding him of the ways he's annoyed me. The first time was when he'd noticed me in town, changing a wheel. I was doing fine. OK, I might have looked awkward, but that was just because I had on my lovely new pink dress and I was being careful not to spoil it.

"Come on, Lizzie. You let me do that," he'd said. "It'll be easier for me and we don't want you getting your pretty dress dirty."

He'd then proceeded to fetch a ridiculously large jack and wheel brace and quickly changed the wheel. I'd had to thank him, of course.

"Think nothing of it, Lizzie. That's what we're here for."

The arrogant man had even had the nerve to wink, before swaggering off.

The next time things had gone badly was at Sheila's house. She was always trying to 'tactfully' leave us together. On that occasion, she'd asked us to mind the kids while she popped down to the corner shop. We'd chatted quite pleasantly until the youngest boy, Sam, had been stung by a wasp and started screaming. Dave just picked the child up and handed him to me.

"There you go, Lizzie. Your department I believe."

Of course I sorted the little chap out, but I noted Dave's view of the world. Cars are men's work, children are where women came in handy.

Dave keeps trying to speak as I remind him of his faults. He rubs his face against his shoulder, trying to work the tape free. This makes his Stetson hat fall off. Hmm, a big strong man like him didn't even put up enough of a fight for his hat to be knocked off.

I've said all I want and am fed up with being shut in here, so decide it's time to release him. First I untie his hands. It's not exactly difficult, surely he could have worked that knot free on his own? He puts his hand up to his face and touches the strip of black tape.

"Oh no you don't. I think you'll find I'm better at that than you are," I say.

This reminds me so much of the annoying patients who come in for jabs or to have wounds dressed. I'd never hurt them on purpose, but sometimes I'm not sorry when it smarts a little. I catch hold of the tape and rip it off in one smooth tug.

"Ouch!"

"Good."

"You don't like me much do you?"

"Nope."

"Why not?" he has the nerve to ask.

"I thought I'd just explained." I can't believe the man; he just won't accept that a woman can resist him.

"You said something about my male chauvinist attitude, but I thought I was just being sensible."

"Not sexist?"

"No. I'm sure you could have changed that wheel, but you were wearing such a nice dress it seemed silly for you to ruin it. Besides, as I work in a garage, I'm used to changing tyres and it's much easier with the proper tools."

"Ah."

"And you're a nurse, I knew you'd be better at dealing with a hurt child. I'd probably have frightened him by making a fuss. You soon calmed him down."

"Ah."

He handed me my hat.

"Come on, partner, put this on. How about we talk about this over a drink once we've got out of here?"

"OK, as long as you've got a plan for that?"

"Yep." He strides to the door and yells, "Sam, if you and the other Indians release us, I'll buy you all an ice cream."

The boys start up their awful war cries again as they rush to unlock the door.

16. All For The Best

I've known Melanie forever. She's the most fun person I've ever met. We learned to ride bikes together, fly kites, throw snowballs. We weren't bad kids, but sometimes we played too loudly or where we weren't supposed to be, helped ourselves to strawberries down the allotments or skimmed our Frisbee close to someone's window. Melanie made our 'victims' laugh with her outlandish excuses so we always got away with it.

She was the first girl I ever kissed – and the last. For her, I was the first of a long string of boyfriends. She never neglected her mate Simon for one of them though, not until Stuart. He didn't like me much. I didn't like him either, but pretended I did for Melanie. What mattered was whether they'd be happy together.

"Are you sure he's the one?" was the closest I came to voicing my doubts.

"Absolutely. I love him and he loves me and besides, he's sensible enough for the pair of us. I need that, don't I?"

I wasn't sure she did. Perhaps I should have said so.

Later I joked, "Can I be your bridesmaid?"

"Of course you can, Simon. Did I mention the colour scheme is puce and I'll want you in a drop-waisted rayon number with bat wing sleeves? Very seventies."

I shuddered. "I was thinking more of something sleek and classic in powder blue silk."

"Not a chance. Can't have you looking prettier than me."

Stuart didn't laugh at our banter. He didn't even give that tight little smile of his.

I wore a sensible suit and went on my own. It was that kind of wedding. Subdued. I had to keep looking at her in all that cream lace to remind myself it really was Melanie's wedding and not that of another, much less exuberant, girl.

Melanie and I didn't see each other much afterwards, but kept in touch on Facebook and with cards at Christmas and birthdays. She phoned me sometimes, always when Stuart was out I realised, but didn't say. We chatted about nothing and giggled for ages. I called her too but she said little and laughed not at all when he was home. I mentioned that to my partner, Julian.

"Maybe she doesn't want to make her husband jealous?" he suggested.

"Oh. Are you jealous... when I talk to her?"

"Now he asks!" His smile assured me he wasn't.

The last time I actually saw Melanie, before I went down there, was when I married Julian. Stuart couldn't make it, apparently, so Melanie came up by train. She'd agreed to be my matron of honour. The trouble I had finding something in puce with bat wing sleeves! The look on her face was worth it though.

Then I showed her the blue silk. "Gotcha, didn't I?"

She laughed. That uncontrollable laughter that leaves a girl's mascara two inches below her eyes.

"Oh, Simon, I haven't laughed properly in ages."

I could well believe it; Stuart never provoked me to hilarity. It was a shame though. I'd hoped that slightly disapproving air was just a reaction to me, not his normal attitude to his gorgeous, bubbly wife.

"And you're still not jealous of my friendship with her?" I asked Julian.

"No, because I want her to be my friend too. Why don't we invite her and her husband to come stay when we get back from honeymoon?"

"I've tried before," I pointed out.

"Try again, things might be different now we're official."

I did. They weren't.

Then she called me. If it hadn't been for caller display I'd not have known it was her.

"Melanie, what's happened? Are you hurt? Ill?"

"He's gone," she sort of whimpered.

"Stuart?" Although who else could she have meant?

She spoke words but they made no sense to me. Probably didn't to her either.

"I'll come down. Right now."

Julian had been watching me during the call and said he'd drive me. It meant he'd have to miss a concert he'd been looking forward to.

"A friend's need is more important," he said.

I cried then. Grief for Melanie mixed with love for him.

On the journey we speculated about what could have happened.

"An accident of some sort?" Julian suggested. "If he'd been ill surely she'd have said something?"

"I don't know. She's rung me a few times lately and interrupted before I could ask after him. Maybe she knew something was wrong."

I was right about that last bit, but not about Stuart. He wasn't dead, just gone as she'd said. Left her for a woman who took things seriously.

"Bitch took stealing my husband so seriously she got pregnant," Melanie spat out, though it had taken a lot of hugs and soothing words to get her calm enough to speak about it.

Once her anger faded, I saw that's all that had been holding her together. She dissolved into the kind of sobbing mess I guessed I'd be in were Julian to leave me. I held her while she cried.

"What can we do?" I whispered to Julian.

"Nothing for her pain, I don't suppose. She'll need practical help though, won't she?"

I nodded. Melanie's not one for practicalities even when her heart isn't broken.

We sat with her while she phoned her family and broke the news. They wanted to help, of course.

"Simon's with me. Julian too."

It was agreed that we'd stay until the end of the week, then her parents would come down. Julian helped her find a solicitor, begin divorce proceedings and work out her finances. Looking forward seemed to help her a little.

"I won't be able to keep this house," she said after looking at Julian's figures. "I'll need something cheaper."

"There are some nice apartments in town, I saw them advertised in the estate agent's window," Julian suggested. "Or maybe you'd rather come home?"

"Home?" she asked.

"Of course that's what you should do, Mels," I said. "Find somewhere near us and your parents and brother."

She actually smiled. Not a proper Melanie grin, but it was definitely a smile. "Maybe I will."

Melanie's parents didn't stay long. Just enough time to help pack a few things and take her back home with them. She soon started job and house hunting by day and cooking meals for her friends and family by night. She joined a book club, walked neighbours' dogs and gave a pretty good impression of being happy.

"She isn't though, is she?" I asked Julian.

"Not yet. Give it time."

There wasn't time though. At least that's how it seemed to me. Stuart called and said she must meet him at their old home to decide who would get what before it was sold.

"I can't do it," she sobbed. "I can't meet him and agree to him taking our things back to... to her."

"Then don't," Julian said.

"What?" Melanie and I both asked together. Julian's the sensible, do the right thing however hard it is, however much it hurts, one. We're the ones who try to wriggle out of difficult situations.

"Why should you do it? It might be what he wants, but you don't have to do what he wants."

"No, not any more," Melanie agreed.

"Is there anything there you really want, other than your share of the money when it's sold?" I asked.

"A few things. There are flower vases that belonged to Granny and things I've been given for birthdays and a few books."

"Nothing valuable? Nothing that he'd think was his?" Julian asked.

"No. I won't want reminders."

"Then you tell him you're going, without him, to collect those things and he can keep everything else. If he doesn't like it his solicitor can contact yours to arrange an alternative distribution."

"Oooh, I like it!" She hugged Julian then practised that little speech until she was able to ring Stuart and deliver it with cool detachment.

I shivered, hoping I'd never hear such words said to me. Julian squeezed my hand and I believed I never would.

Melanie wasn't so cool when I went with her to collect her things. Her treasures were mixed in with what had once been their treasures. A dried carnation from his wedding buttonhole, photos and wedding gifts.

Tears filled Melanie's eyes as she discovered a bottle of champagne. "It's the one you and Julian had delivered to our hotel on the wedding night. I'd hidden a half full one wrapped up in my veil when we left the reception so we drank that and kept yours for a special occasion."

I was angry. Not that they'd not drunk it that night, but that it was still unopened.

"Three years of marriage and you never had a reason to open it?"

"No," Melanie whispered.

"Really? Not a single moment worthy of a glass of wine?"

"Apparently not."

"So, can you explain why you're crying over him leaving?"

She stared at me. Not surprising as those were probably the harshest words I've ever said to her. Hard as it was, I knew I must continue showing she was crying over losing something she'd never really had.

I remembered something I'd noticed in her bathroom on my previous visit and fetched the dusty bottle of perfume.

"How long have you had this?"

"Stuart bought it for my birthday."

"Which was almost a year ago."

"Yes." She looked puzzled.

"He bought you perfume you don't like?"

"I do like it."

"But it's almost full." My Melanie, the Melanie before Stuart, always smelled gorgeous even if we were just going for a mooch round a car boot sale.

"I was saving it for best," Melanie explained.

"Best? Hmm let me guess, very few best times to wear it?"

"That's right. Well no, we had good times."

"And you'll have more without him. Perhaps some so good they'll seem worth putting on a squirt of perfume for."

She glared at me, but there were no more tears as she searched for the items she'd come to collect. We wrapped them and stowed them in the boot of my car.

"Anything else?" I asked.

"I might as well take my clothes."

"And those nice leather suitcases to put them in?" I suggested.

She gave a tiny grin. "Why not? He bought them for a holiday we never took. He had too many business trips to fit it in. At least I thought they were business trips." The grin faded, but was replaced by a look of determination, not desperation.

I pulled out hangers and held them up for her 'yes' or 'no'. I was pleased all the brightest items got a yes. She actually laughed when I held up the puce dress with bat wing sleeves.

"I told Stuart that's what I'd worn. You should have seen his face!"

I smiled too and put it on the 'no' pile.

Melanie shook her head. "I want to keep it."

As I packed up the clothes, shoes and accessories she was keeping, Melanie turned her attention to her underwear drawer. Rather a lot of sensible, slightly greying knickers joined the 'no' heap. A few pretty silky things were added to the 'yes' items.

"You'll not be surprised to hear those haven't been worn much," she said; bitterly I thought.

Once everything was packed into the car I squeezed her shoulder. "Well done. Come on; I'll treat you to lunch and a big glass of wine."

"Thanks, Si." She hugged me. "Hold on just a sec." She ran back into the house and came out carrying two bottles. The perfume and champagne. "This lunch... going somewhere nice are we?"

"The best pub between here and home," I assured her.

She gave herself a couple of generous squirts of perfume.

When I dropped her back at her new home she hugged me. "Thanks for lunch and well, everything."

"What are friends for?" I asked.

"They should be for fun stuff, not this?" She gestured to the cases in her hallway.

"OK then. Think of something fun and we'll do that."

She rose to the challenge much sooner than I'd expected.

"There's an open air concert next Friday. Not one of those posh dos Julian likes I'm afraid but the kind with fireworks and burger vans. I thought we could try and glam it up a bit though. Posh frocks, a fancy picnic and champagne."

"Sounds like a plan!"

When I consulted with Julian he readily agreed. "I'm sure we can bring a welcome touch of class to the event."

It wasn't until he marked it on the calendar I realised the date of the concert was also Melanie's wedding anniversary.

I suspect Melanie is a bad influence on Julian because he insisted we both wear evening dress with hideously bright waistcoats and cravats. He took a candelabra, china plates and a huge linen tablecloth to use as a picnic blanket.

Melanie wore the puce dress, of course, and lots of perfume. I'm not one to spend much time thinking about women's underwear but I imagined hers would be pretty silk, not grey cotton. The meal began with us peeling prawns, by candlelight. It continued with a whole roasted chicken she insisted we refer to, loudly, as pheasant and finished with chocolate covered strawberries. The fireworks were illuminating the sky and our laughing faces by then.

We drank champagne too. Not the bottle Julian and I had given her exactly four years before.

"I'd decided to drink it on the very next special occasion so planned to have it tonight," she explained.

"It's OK if you're not quite ready," I said. "I'm sure you will be soon."

"You don't understand. I've already drunk it. You see the toilet roll holder in my new bathroom broke." She paused but Julian and I said nothing. "And I'm hopelessly impractical aren't I?"

Again we said nothing.

"So I phoned my brother and asked him to come round and put up a new one. Then I went out and bought one. I got out the emergency tool kit Dad optimistically bought me and found the screwdriver. By the time Bill got there I'd fixed it up and thrown the old one away. He said I'd made a good job of it."

"Go on," I encouraged.

"I couldn't remember the last time I'd coped with anything on my own. I'll probably never need to as I've got you guys and Bill and Mum and Dad, so doing something that one time felt like a special occasion. Bill and I sat on my bathroom floor and drank champagne from mugs."

"What a Melanie thing to do," I laughed.

"Then, as I knew tonight would be a special occasion too, I bought another bottle."

"This one is absolutely delicious, so I think it's all worked out for the best," Julian said.

We drank to that.

I could still see the laughter sparkling in Melanie's eyes after we'd blown out the candles.

17. The Wrong Woman

Stacey wasn't who she wanted to be. She'd become an old and useless nobody. Older and more useless anyway. A lot more useless, perhaps not that much older. She wasn't sure how long she'd been in the coma. They probably told her, but they'd told her so many things.

They'd told her about her legs, the chair, the crash. A car crash, that's right. Now she remembered. She'd been walking, she could walk then, and a car had hit her and spun her in the air. She'd landed a different woman; a grey-skinned nobody. A woman who couldn't walk, or talk or even breathe without the help of a machine. She was the wrong woman. This shouldn't have happened to her.

"Three months," the nurse said when Stacey asked how long she'd been in hospital.

Only three months? It seemed so much longer, lying there with nothing to do but think. She'd thought she'd die and of all the things she'd never done. She'd done a lot of thinking. Windsurfing, karaoke and paint-balling were things she'd never tried and now never could. To be honest, they were things she didn't really want to do. Poetry though and flower arranging and... so many other things she had wanted to attempt. She'd been too scared she'd look a fool if she couldn't do them well.

Stacey thought of chances she'd wasted. No driving lessons in case she failed the test. Holidays in England as she was afraid to fly. The same job since leaving school because trying for another might mean being turned down at interview.

There were other things she hadn't done. She hadn't told David she loved him. Wouldn't take the risk that he might not care so much about her as she did about him. Tears rolled down her face. Now she was crippled and wouldn't be given another chance to say it.

He'd told her everyday at her hospital bedside.

"Please wake up, Stacey," he'd whispered again and again. "You don't have to love me, just squeeze my hand. Or blink, can you blink?"

She couldn't squeeze his hand and she couldn't blink. She could only listen and love. She could have said she loved him; if she could have talked.

In the coma she'd thought of marriage and motherhood. Friends, hobbies and interests. Things she could one day have tried. Things she wouldn't have attempted. She couldn't admit she wanted them, wanted them with David. Now it didn't matter what she wanted. She'd known he'd get tired of her eventually, the accident meant she didn't have to wait.

Her new wrong body was good. No one would expect her to achieve anything now. She could stay living at home with her parents. They couldn't now tell her she was quite capable of looking after herself.

"You're diabetic, that's all," her dad had snapped when she'd tried to explain things weren't easy for her.

He didn't know what it was like. People didn't avoid him because he had to stick needles into himself twice a day.

He said it wasn't true. "You could try to make friends."

She could have tried. Should have, but had preferred not to risk rejection.

"Come on then, let's get you out of that bed," a nurse said, interrupting Stacey's thoughts.

"Why?"

"Physio."

She remembered. They said they'd work her muscles, teach her to be independent in a special chair. She was the wrong woman. They should give their time and energy to someone who could be helped. Someone who hadn't wasted her life so far and was now forced to waste the rest.

"There's no point," Stacey said. "I can't do anything." Even as she said it, Stacey dared to hope it wasn't true.

"Not yet," the nurse agreed. "Your muscles are wasted. We'll get them going again."

"But my legs..."

"No, we can't get them going as well as they did before, but there's still lots you can do."

"Like what?"

"You can squeeze my hand," David said.

He'd come back. Yesterday she'd told him she was the wrong woman for him, but he'd come back. He held her hand and she didn't try to pull it away.

"You'll be able to sit at a desk and use a keyboard, so there'll be plenty of jobs you can do. You could learn to drive an adapted car. Maybe take up a sport with the right chair. You'll be able to kiss me and quite a bit more. There's no reason why we shouldn't have a family if you manage your diabetes correctly. First though, you have to try to do the exercises. Will you try?"

"Yes." She squeezed David's hand. She'd show everyone, herself included, she was the right woman; a person worth loving.

18. Can We Just Stop?

"Can we stop? I'd like to take a picture."

Eva photographed a pretty thatched house, which had plants growing on the roof, as Graham checked his watch.

Oh dear, would the whole holiday be like this? As the ferry arrived in St Malo she'd caught tantalising glimpses of the old town. She'd have loved to explore, but they'd driven straight to their first hotel. Admittedly it wasn't a long drive and the scenery was lovely, but again she'd caught only glimpses as they passed by.

In Dinan they'd walked up steep cobbled streets and along ramparts, visited the Chateau Musee, Jardin Anglaise and St Saviour's Basilica. They'd seen the impressive viaduct over the River Rance and a church with amazing stained glass windows. They'd taken a boat trip and eaten at a quayside restaurant. Despite the hectic pace she'd loved it all.

He'd gone through their schedule over breakfast that morning, reminding Eva they were going from Rouen up through Normandy to Calvados and the Overlord beaches, then spending two days in Paris before heading down to Fountainbleu's picturesque forest and Palace. As Graham talked about the delights of La Rochelle and the traditional Breton buildings in Quimper, Eva had felt queasy. It could just have been the dizzying thought of doing all that in nine days, but she was almost certain it was something else.

Graham's schedule would be as frantic as their normal lives, where there wasn't time to stop and think or just to stop. She'd have liked to look in one of the patisseries or wander around a quaint village or anything but this relentless push to... to what? They couldn't see the whole of France in one trip.

As Graham restarted the car, and the satnav reminded him to drive on the right, she tried to explain.

"You'd like to see the real France, not just tourist spots?" Graham suggested.

"Sort of." She wanted to see the real Graham. The normal man under the need to do more, achieve and acquire more. She didn't dare say so; what if there wasn't one?

What if things only got worse after she told him her news? Eva was almost certainly pregnant. She'd wanted to savour the idea, rather than rush straight into making more plans, so hadn't said a word.

Eva sighed. He'd become more driven than ever to build a good life for the child. She knew the history. Graham's great-great-grandfather started the business, great-grandfather kept it going through the depression, grandad built it up into a success, father expanded and diversified. Graham felt obliged to top that; but could it be done and did it need to be? The company was thriving and they already had a nice home. It wasn't a mansion, just an ordinary family home and she'd like them to live in it as an ordinary family. Wasn't that good enough for Graham? Or was it her, was she too ordinary? She must stop that. It was just hormones making her emotional.

Graham would be an excellent father, just as he was an excellent husband. Excellent except hardly ever there. That's why she hadn't yet told him about the baby. She was determined to do it when he actually stopped for a minute and could listen.

An awful screech and the feeling of the car lurching to the

side of the road interrupted her thoughts.

"Must be a puncture," Graham said once he'd brought the car to a stop in the verge. "Eva? Are you OK?"

"It was just a bit of a shock." For a moment it had seemed she'd somehow caused this with her wish to stop.

"I'd better put up a warning triangle for other motorists," Graham said.

After a few minutes watching her husband struggling, and failing, to undo the wheel nuts she asked, "Should I call the breakdown people?"

"I think you'd better."

Between Eva's evening class French and the other lady's rather better English the situation was soon understood.

"Are you alone?"

Eva glanced across the street to where white painted chairs waited invitingly outside a patisserie and made it clear she and her husband had somewhere comfortable to wait and no urgent appointment to keep.

"About two hours," she told Graham. "They'll call when they're close."

"Better make the most of the time here then."

Just as she feared a frenzied dash round the locality, in search of some enriching experience, he added, "You said you fancied an aimless wander and to try a coffee and cake?"

"Won't it mess up your schedule if we eat now?"

Graham shrugged. "It's already messed up. Might as well accept it."

"So you can relax if you're forced into it?"

He grinned. "There's something in that. The puncture

wasn't our fault so it's not our fault if we just tread water here for a bit."

"And the holiday wasn't your fault either. You only agreed to take one because your wife insisted?"

"Er... yes."

"Is your dad really such a tyrant? He doesn't seem that way to me."

"No, not a tyrant at all. He's always been a great father when he was there. He pushed us all to be the best we could and never waste an opportunity or a minute... Sorry that's probably why I went overboard on the whole scheduling thing. I know we don't spend enough time together and wanted to make the most of it."

"Like your dad did with you?"

"Yes. We went to some brilliant places and did exciting things. Although to be honest I wished sometimes he'd just stop for a minute and mess about playing games with us like ordinary families. Not that I'm criticising Dad. He's done what every generation of the family has done but..."

"And when we have a baby?"

"I'd want the very best for him or her."

"Even if that means stopping and messing about sometimes?"

"Yes, yes it does. Perhaps I need to practise?" He fetched the schedule and ripped it in two.

Was that the perfect moment to tell him? Maybe, but there was no need to make the most of every such moment. There would be more to come.

19. What's Your Sign?

"Thank you, Sharon. That was lovely," Janet said.

The girl flushed and sat down.

"Would anyone like to say anything about Sharon's poem?"

Sharon looked as nervous as Janet felt. Thankfully, no one called any rude comments and a few pupils raised a hand.

"Yes, Noah?"

"Were all right. Rhymed and that."

"Yes, the rhymes were excellent, weren't they? Yes, Sally?"

"Bit about the sunset sounded pretty."

"Yes it did. Your images were very clear, Sharon."

"Bit poncey," one boy called. "All lovey dovey."

Sharon looked like she might cry.

"Too gentle for you, Tyrone?" Janet asked. "Well then, we'll expect something really dramatic and exciting from you when you read yours next week."

Tyrone scowled.

"Philip, did you have something to say?"

"Well, it sounded like a real poem, like what they read in plays an' stuff."

"I think that's because it has very good rhythm, it flows easily," Janet suggested.

Philip nodded.

"Well, Sharon has set a very high standard, but I'm sure

the rest of you will also produce something interesting for us. You don't have to use the same style as Sharon and your subject can be anything you like."

"Anything, Miss?"

"Yes, Tyrone. Anything at all as long as it really is a poem and you write it yourself."

As a reward for reasonably good behaviour, Janet dismissed 3b early. "Be quiet, I don't want you disturbing classes which haven't finished yet."

Janet headed for the staff room, hoping to get a few minutes alone with Geoff, who had a free period.

He looked up and smiled as she walked in. His smile was so warm, she could almost convince herself he was as pleased to see her as she was to see him.

"Didn't eat you then, 3b?"

"No, they really are getting better. Nobody at all got bitten today."

"Wow! I'm impressed."

"I need a coffee though. You want one?"

"Got one thanks," he said indicating his full mug.

What was wrong with her? She could persuade the likes of Sharon and Philip to express themselves about poetry yet she couldn't have a simple conversation with Geoff without saying something daft.

Maybe if he didn't do that cute thing with his eyebrow whenever he spoke to her it would be easier?

Janet grabbed a magazine, sat opposite Geoff and pretended to read.

"What's so interesting?" he asked.

Her acting must be better than she thought. She took a

proper look at the page. "My horoscope."

"Don't tell me you believe all that rubbish?"

"Well, it's a bit generalised, but sometimes it's accurate." She scanned the entry for Virgo. "It says here that a close friend is going to get a surprise."

Janet stood, took two paces toward Geoff intending to playfully swipe him with the magazine. As she approached, he leapt to his feet and somehow, instead of the magazine brushing his head, her lips brushed his cheek.

Janet backed away quickly.

"Are we the same sign then? You look as surprised as me," Geoff said.

"Er, yes, no. Um... sorry." She sat down again.

"No problem. What does it say for me then?"

"Your ruler Mars is showing you how to achieve your dreams. The seventeenth is a good day to take decisive action."

"Hmmm, the seventeenth is the school fete. I assume you'll be going?"

"It's pretty much compulsory."

"Then I look forward to seeing you there and to acting decisively."

Philip's poem was about the death of his dog. It didn't scan very well, but the awkwardness added to the sentiment. Not one child said anything rude or flippant. Sharon admitted it made her want to cry and even Tyrone said, "Sad that."

Tyrone's own poem didn't rhyme, but if he'd wanted rhyming words he could have used 'duck', 'quit' and 'very well'. It was angry and raw, but it was a poem and Janet felt he'd worked at putting down what he meant to say, rather than just scribbling the first rude words which occurred to him.

"I never knew you could swear in a poem!" Sharon said.

"It's not usual, but in this case it works rather well."

"And it means I can say it in class without getting detention," Tyrone pointed out.

There was a lively debate about how poetry allowed people to say things they wouldn't normally feel able to express. Maybe she should write one to Geoff?

"I'm very impressed," Janet said. "You've all managed to create an original poem and have expressed yourselves in different ways, not just in your own work, but when discussing other people's. I think we should also allow more people to read these poems. I'd like to put them on display at the school fete."

"No, Miss; you can't!" her pupils cried almost in unison.

"Why not?"

She discovered that though they quite liked the idea of people reading their work, they felt they'd be embarrassed if others knew they were the authors.

"How about we print them out anonymously?"

There were a few tentative nods.

"You could all type them up on the computer and include suitable illustrations, then we could add some of the comments you made when they were read. There could be space underneath for people to add their own thoughts too. At the end, if you wanted to, you could then fill in the names of the authors."

The class agreed to her plan and were very enthusiastic about selecting fonts and graphics for their work.

When she displayed the class's efforts, Janet would also include one of her own poems. She allowed her pupils to illustrate it and add their own feedback.

"Can I give you a hand with that?" Geoff asked as she carried the printed sheets into the hall.

"Thanks." Janet really couldn't help it that their hands brushed often and they occasionally had to put an arm across each other's shoulders as they arranged the poems and pinned them up.

"Bit brave isn't it? Allowing people to say what they think?"

"Maybe, but I'm going to keep an eye on things and edit feedback if necessary."

"I hope you're going to have time to get your fortune told?"

"Wouldn't miss it for anything." Janet laughed, she knew as well as he did that the drama club, which he led, were doing the readings.

"Great. I'll come and get you when, er, when it's a good time."

"Thank you." She laughed again. It seemed fairly clear he had somebody particular in mind to do her reading. She just hoped it wasn't Tyrone.

The 'gypsy' really was very convincing, if she hadn't known it was Sharon from 3b, whom she'd seen giggling with Geoff, and later Tyrone, she might have been fooled.

"Sit yourself down, Miss, er I mean Missy and cross my palm with silver," Sharon cackled.

Janet handed over coins until Sharon decided the mists

were beginning to clear.

"It's a special day today, a day for love," Sharon said. "Poetry will show the way."

"I hope so."

"Me too, er, I mean, I know so, it's written in the stars."

"How will I know?"

"Look out for the letter G. That will bring love."

Very weird. Could Sharon really know her secret?

When everyone but the helpers had left, Janet returned to her poetry board for a last look at the work and comments, before packing them away. Sharon's love poem was marked with the letter G. Under it, Tyrone had added a hand-written comment. 'Sorry I was rude about this in class. It's good, really I wished it was about me.'

That explained a lot, not least Tyrone's recent decision to join the drama club.

"Do you think it is?" Geoff whispered in her ear.

Janet jumped. "I didn't notice you there! Sorry, what did you say?"

"The poem, it's Sharon's isn't it?"

"Yes."

"Do you think it really is about Tyrone?"

"I rather think it might be... unless you gave her the lines to say during the readings?"

"No, they wrote their own. I made a few suggestions, but... Why, what did she say?"

"Oh, stuff about tonight being the time for love."

"I see." He looked thoughtful. "Who wrote this one?" Geoff asked, pointing to the poem marked K; Janet's own work.

"Er, I did."

"Can I borrow a pen?"

Janet gave him one.

He wrote, 'Sorry I was rude about horoscopes, I hope I was wrong and they're accurate, just as I hope this poem is about me.'

"Do you think it is?" Janet whispered in his ear.

"I rather think it might be, but I know how to find out." He kissed her.

Janet heard a door bang shut. She and Geoff stepped apart and turned to see Tyrone and Sharon on the opposite side of the hall. Janet didn't know if they'd seen her and Geoff kissing, but guessed not as they were holding hands and gazing into each other's eyes.

20. With Arty Kisses

Kirstey Swithas watched Mr Davies stride away down the corridor. She and half the school had a crush on him. The possible exception was Miss Daniels, the deputy head, but she was positively ancient!

Mr Davies never seemed to notice Kirstey. "Morning, girls," he'd say and smile as he passed her and her friends. She was just one of the crowd to him. She'd done her best to get noticed; shortening her navy blue skirt, swapping her usual sensible white blouse for something low cut and lacy and putting up her hair in a rough approximation of Amy Winehouse on a good day. Immediately after each slight change of look, Miss Daniels had a quiet word with Kirstey and impressed upon her the need to dress appropriately.

"Sorry, Miss Daniels," she'd said, feeling about nine years old and resisting the temptation to stick her tongue out behind the woman's back.

Miss Daniels might be able to censure her dress, but there was nothing that battleaxe could do about her mail. Mr Davies was going to receive a Valentine's card which would make him want to know more about the sender. Kirstey, who's very good at art, was making it herself. The picture was easy; Mr Davies lived in a beautiful cottage on the edge of the village green. It had a wonderful view of willow trees, a duck pond and rolling hills in the background. Kirstey hadn't been stalking him or anything, she just happened to see his details on some paperwork during a recent school trip and had then cycled through the village a week later. One break-time she'd managed to get him into conversation and casually mentioned her trip.

He'd admitted he lived there and said it inspired his poetry. Kirstey made a sketch of his beloved view and transformed it into a card. The inside of the card presented more of a problem. He was an English teacher who wrote his own poems, so might appreciate her writing one. Unfortunately, Kirstey wasn't very good at English, especially poetry. Her first effort was quickly rejected.

You've captured my heart

Dear darling Mr Davies

You're like a piece of art,

I want to have your babies.

Although it rhymed, it was definitely rushing things so might scare him off.

Her other attempts were even worse. Perhaps she could borrow one from someone else? Someone obscure, in the hope of passing it off as her own? An internet search produced some wonderfully romantic verses, but Kirstey wasn't sure exactly how obscure the authors really were. Just because she'd never heard of them was no guarantee that Mr Davies wouldn't recognise the words. Maybe she should go for a well-known classic?

Shall I compare thee to a Summer's day?

Thou art more lovely and more temperate:

No, although it was beautiful and romantic, it was more suitable for a woman.

I wandered lonely as a cloud

That floats on high o'er vales and hills.

Lovely and it did go on to mention lakes and trees and things, but the mention of loneliness might make her seem desperate.

Maybe something from a song would be better?

She didn't know if he was a 5 Seconds of Summer fan though; surprisingly, not everyone was. Probably best just to sign it with kisses. That was it! She put her artistic abilities to good use and signed it 'with arty kisses'. After dropping the card into his tutor group's register she tried to forget about it.

After lunch, she found a card on her desk in the art room.

"Did anyone see who left this?" she asked as she opened it.

The card was a bought one, but very pretty. Inside it said,

Shall I compare thee to a Summer's day?

Thou art more lovely and more temperate:

"Come on, someone must have seen who left this. I'll give five house points to whoever tells me."

"We can't do that, Miss Swithas. Mr Davies promised ten each if we kept quiet."

"Mr Davies did?"

"Yes," said a deep voice behind her. "Fortunately, I'm better at anagrams than I am at bribery, Kirstey."

He covered Kirstey Swithas with arty kisses, but not until break-time, after she'd dismissed her class.

21. Good Looking With Bacon

"Thanks, Susie, see you next week," said her attractive customer.

Since she'd started work on the checkout, Susie had got used to strangers addressing her by name, but was still pleasantly surprised 'Mr Good Looking With Bacon' had bothered to read her badge. Usually it was elderly customers who took the trouble to learn her name. Susie was always pleased to share a few words of cheerful chit-chat with them. She'd never win the prize for the fastest checkout operator, but there was more to life than that. Susie was always pleased to chit-chat with good looking young men too, but the supermarket didn't have many customers in that category. Not that it mattered, one would be enough, provided he was the right man.

Susie had liked the look of him and his shopping trolley the first time she'd served him. Just about enough food to last a single person for a week, she guessed.

"Sorry for the wait," she'd said.

"No problem, I'm not in a hurry," he'd told her.

She hoped he'd been admiring the view, of her, as he'd waited.

"Would you like any help with your packing?" she'd asked even though he only had a few items; it was company policy.

"I'm fine, but thanks for asking."

He was more than fine.

A lot could be learnt about people by their shopping habits. The sweet old ladies who bought the own-brand labels and reduced priced items for themselves and six tins of the most expensive cat or dog food on the market always spoke pleasantly to her. The people buying themselves the most expensive products were usually the ones who made the most complaints and were rudest. Money didn't buy manners or happiness it seemed. Some fit healthy people bought lots of fresh produce, but others bought none. Susie wondered if they had an allotment and grew their own.

Susie doubted her own trolley revealed much about her. True, it contained her favourite caramel and chocolate biscuits, but who was to know? They were buried under the digestives her dad liked, her brother's custard creams and rusks for her little sister. That showed she came from a family of biscuit eaters, but that's not exactly uncommon. Maybe someone counting the number of packs and noting they were all from the luxury range might guess she'd been working in the store long enough to be entitled to staff discount. She hoped people, especially young good looking male people, might see her as more than a thoughtful family member and reliable checkout operator.

She deduced her good looking customer was very fond of bacon sandwiches. Susie guessed he ate them for breakfast every day and occasionally fantasised about preparing them for him. One thing she couldn't guess was his name. He could read hers easily enough, on his receipt as well as her badge, but unless customers paid by cheque, she couldn't learn theirs. That's why she and the other girls thought of customers in terms of their purchases.

"Giant cheese pizza and diet Coke man was in again today," or "Lady organic everything is complaining the lemon grass was too tough," for example.

Every week the attractive bacon buyer came to her till. That had to mean something, didn't it? Every week he made a comment about the weather, or a special offer. He noticed when she took a week off and asked her if she'd had a nice time. Once he mentioned a pub he drank in. Susie had persuaded her friends to go there for an evening, but she hadn't seen him. She tried to think of a way of letting him know where she went in the evenings, but after that one time, it wasn't something that often came up in conversation.

Then he started to buy muesli instead of bacon. Everyone is entitled to a change of breakfast, but the addition of sweeteners, toilet fresheners and scented candles and an increase in the food quantities suggested he was no longer breakfasting alone. Susie's breakfast fantasy turned to thoughts of a girl burning her hair on the candles and choking on flakes of whole-grain. She tried to put those thoughts out her mind. It wasn't the girl's fault she'd got the man Susie wanted and it wasn't Good Looking With Bacon's fault that he didn't feel about Susie the way she felt about him.

One day as she scanned his muesli, he asked, "Do you like muesli, Susie?"

"It's OK, but not as nice as a bacon butty," she'd told him.

He'd smiled, but it hadn't reached his eyes.

After a few weeks, he was back to bacon.

"Gone off muesli?" she asked as casually as possible.

"No, gone off the girl who ate it."

So she'd been right and now he was single again.

"Actually, that's not exactly true."

For a moment, she thought he'd read her mind, but then she saw his thoughts were all his own and none of them were happy.

"I'm on my break in a minute, would you like a coffee?" she said before her brain had time to decide if that was a good idea.

"Thanks, I'll put this in the car and come back."

So she'd bought two coffees in the store's cafe and learnt his name was Richard and the muesli eater was Tanya and that Tanya was beautiful and clever and preferred someone called Charles who probably gave her caviar for breakfast. Richard hadn't felt like eating and had only bought the food for the chance to see Susie's friendly smile. Susie was a nice person, he said. Nothing about beautiful and clever though.

They chatted more after that. Richard would heap everything on the belt as quickly as he could, then stand near her, packing the items very slowly as they talked about the weather, TV programmes and eventually evenings out, so she was able to mention her local pub.

He turned up at The Frog and Bucket the following Friday.

"My round," he said. "I'm afraid it never occurred to me to pay you for coffee the other week." He bought drinks for Susie and her friends.

"Oh, I didn't realise you two had a thing going," one of her friends said.

He didn't deny it. He joked with her friends and agreed that Susie did indeed 'scrub up well' once out of her supermarket uniform, but he left before she'd finished her drink and could offer to buy him one.

He was even more friendly after that and sometimes complimented her on her hair or asked after her friends. When she saw him approaching with a bunch of pink roses sticking out of his trolley, her heart beat a little faster. It soon sank when she saw the flowers were resting on some fancy organic muesli. There was a lot more food than usual, including exotic fruit, fresh fish and white wine. The air fresheners were back too. Susie could only hope this was for the benefit of a new girl and not the heartbreaker Tanya.

It was a new girl. Her name was Rebecca and she was very pretty. To make it worse, she was also very nice. She came shopping with him a couple of times. She chatted to Susie as though they were old friends and it was clear Richard had told Rebecca all about 'that nice girl in the supermarket'.

Susie's breakfast fantasy became a nightmare. She'd be invited to Rebecca and Richard's wedding breakfast and have to smile as they cut the cake and held each other tight for their first dance. She considered asking to be transferred to another branch of the store, so she wouldn't have to smile at Richard and his full trolley, so told her manager she wanted a change.

The thought of not seeing Richard was too much though, so she asked to be transferred to shelf stacking instead. Susie didn't see him at all the following week. Had he not been in or had she just not seen him? She swapped from the tinned goods aisle to the meat aisle. Richard was bound to spot her when he chose his bacon.

Susie was wrong, it was Rebecca she saw looking at the packs of streaked and smokey.

"Excuse me, could you help me?" she called out before Susie could dodge behind the sausages. "Oh, Susie! Am I pleased to see you."

The feeling wasn't at all mutual.

"How can I help?"

"I thought I'd treat Richard to some really good bacon to cheer him up after his accident, but I..."

"Accident? Is he OK?"

"He will be in time. Ironic isn't it, that I've got to start looking after him the week I should have been moving out."

"You're moving out?"

"A girl can't stay with her brother forever, however kind he is to her."

"Brother?"

"If you're anything near as shocked as you look, I think I'd better take you to get some coffee."

In the cafe, Susie learnt that Richard had broken a leg, three ribs and his collarbone, but was out of hospital. She also discovered that some time previously Rebecca had split with her fiancé and moved out of the house they'd shared and into Richard's flat.

"I'd only intended it to be for a few weeks, but he asked me to stay until my ex and I could sell our place and I could use my share of the money on a deposit for somewhere else. He's a really nice person and looked after me so well that it was easy to agree."

Susie could understand that. She'd easily agree to Richard looking after her.

"The house is sold now and I've bought a flat. Richard was helping me move the furniture when he had the accident, so of course I'm looking after him now. Shame he hasn't got a girlfriend to help."

"Shame it's not me," Susie muttered.

"Oh?"

"Crikey, did I say that out loud?"

"Afraid so. Actually, I agree with you and I'm pretty sure Richard would if he were here. But what about your family?"

"I expect they'd be pleased for me. How do you know about them?"

"Richard came in quite late one evening, intending to ask you out and saw you shopping."

"We get a staff discount, I don't see why that would put him off."

"You were buying nappies and men's razors."

"For my little sister and big brother." Susie grinned. "Seems Richard and I both jumped to the wrong conclusion about what was in each other's trolleys."

"You know the truth now. How are we going to break the news to Richard?"

Rebecca finished her shopping without buying any bacon. Susie bought some thick sliced, dry cured premium rashers just before the store closed for the night. The following morning she only had a cup of coffee at home, before going to the address Rebecca had given her. Richard's sister let her in and showed her to the kitchen.

"He prefers it not too crispy and with just a tiny bit of brown sauce," Rebecca said. "I'll leave you to it."

Susie made two sandwiches and a pot of tea, loaded up a tray and carried it in to Richard.

"Susie!" Richard said as she pushed open the door. "Rebecca told me about your conversation yesterday, but she never told me you were coming here."

"Well, she forgot the bacon and I couldn't leave you to try to recover without having a decent breakfast."

He bit into his sandwich.

"Is it OK?" she asked.

"Perfect, and you're my perfect woman."

"I am?"

"Yeah, how could I resist someone good looking with bacon?"

22. Doing The 'Smart' Thing

"Sally, phone call!"

Great timing. "Can you say I'll call back?" she asked without much hope. Angela knew she was getting changed so it must be urgent.

"It's Señor Rodriguez and until Alberto gets back you're the only one here who knows any Spanish."

Sally sighed. If only Alberto were there, and not just because he'd be much better at handling the technical aspects of the call. She'd not seen much of her charismatic colleague recently as he'd been helping out in another office most of the time.

Señor Rodriguez was an important client, one who lately was often impatient. Keeping him waiting wouldn't help matters. Not keeping him waiting probably wouldn't either. They'd met a few times the previous year and got on well, so she'd thought. In person she'd had little trouble with his accent when he spoke English and he'd been charmed by her attempts at Spanish. Over the phone Sally found it difficult to follow much of what he said and had got her pronouns mixed up and referred to him as female. At first they'd laughed at the mix-ups, but after a while he stopped trying to communicate with her and dealt with Alberto. That had been a disappointment to Sally, just one of many. All year she'd been trying hard to do the right thing, but almost all her good intentions had backfired. Her life was in a rut; a deep dark one which just went round in circles.

At the Christmas party, three months previously, Sally and

her colleagues had talked about their New Year's resolutions. Sally's had been, 'sort myself out, get a love life and live happily ever after'.

Some people thought those were good plans, but not the person she'd most wanted to impress; her best friend and line manager, Angela.

"They're too vague, Sally. How exactly are you going to sort yourself out? And I'm not sure it's wise to pin all your hopes of future happiness on someone you haven't yet met."

"Not all my hopes," Sally protested, she had met the man her hopes centred around. "But I would like to get married and have children and I can't do that entirely alone." She said the last bit softly, as Alberto was nearby. She'd like her children to have glossy hair and gorgeous dark eyes, very like his but the office party wasn't the place to admit as much.

"What you need to do is make your resolutions S.M.A.R.T.," Angela continued. "You know, Specific, Measurable, Achievable..."

"Realistic and Time related, like on our staff reports?"

"Absolutely."

Maybe Sally should listen. Angela had started work as an office junior straight from school, worked her way up to section head, married the boy she'd started dating at fifteen and had two sweet children. She was so content with her life she'd have been in danger of seeming smug if it weren't for her being such a nice person and the way she wanted her friends to be equally happy and secure.

Sally had studied hairdressing, switched to media studies after the first term, left before the course finished and had dozens of temping jobs since. Her love life was even worse. Angela had been there for her every time things had gone wrong and helped her get this job. Sally wanted to repay her friend by doing it well. Even her hopes for future happiness were in part to stop Angela being so concerned for her.

"Well, time related is easy; by the end of the year. Is getting fit and learning a bit of Spanish achievable and realistic enough for you?" As she spoke, she watched Alberto dancing. He was fluent in Spanish and English (plus Italian and German). His lithe body and the ease with which he moved suggested he worked out regularly.

"That depends on the specifics. How about aiming to hold a short conversation in Spanish and being able to run for a mile?"

Sally had negotiated that down to travelling a mile under her own steam and exchanging a couple of sentences in Spanish without any terrible misunderstandings. Even to her that sounded like something she could do and they should help towards her real aims of sorting herself out, getting a love life and living happily ever after.

As she reflected on that, Sally zipped up her skirt and strode across the office.

"*Hola, Señor Rodriguez. ¿Como está?*" she asked.

His reply was much longer than the 'bien gracias' her 'teach yourself Spanish' tapes had led her to expect and said much more quickly, but then there were lots of ways to say you were OK and he was probably asking after her health in return.

Deciding not to tell him about her slightly delicate problem, she suddenly had a brilliant idea. Her computer was right there, all she need do was type in what she wanted to say and read it out. "Bueno," she replied, as she typed, 'Alberto is not here. He is in Wales. Please call him there. The number is zero, one...' adding a few more *Buenos* and some *muy buenas* to fill in the pause.

The words, '*Alberto no está aquí. Él está en Gales. Por favor llamarlo allí. El número es cero, uno*...' appeared on her screen and she did her best to read them. She had to repeat herself a couple of times and it was abundantly clear Señor Rodriguez still wasn't charmed by her use of his native tongue, but eventually he'd repeated the numbers back to her, waited for her to say *si* after each and then hung up.

"Oh, well done," Angela said. "That sounded great."

"Actually I'm not sure it did and anyway, I cheated..." she showed Angela the computer screen.

"Oh." Angela read the phrases Sally had typed. "Oh, but Sally..."

"I'm a disaster aren't I?"

In January Sally had got hold of a set of Spanish language tapes and bought a pair of trainers. She also learned cycling was Alberto's exercise of choice. Unfortunately she couldn't afford a bike. By February it was still too cold to go out running, but she had managed to borrow a cassette player so she could listen to the tapes. The very boring tapes.

She'd tried speaking a few words of greeting when Señor Rodriguez called, before switching him through to Alberto, but once the novelty had worn off, the Spaniard was clearly irritated by her halting words and an accent which probably sounded closer to Brummie than Barcelona.

A fortnight ago Sally's parents bought her a reconditioned bicycle for her birthday. She'd ridden it to work a few times. Angela was very understanding about her late arrival on the first attempt. Sally thought she might be able to get used to the earlier starts, but not to being freezing cold or to the way the saddle chafed, which was why she'd bought cycling shorts in her lunch break and was trying them on when

Señor Rodriguez called.

Sally said, "I did try to do your S.M.A.R.T. resolutions, honestly but just like all my good intentions they haven't worked out." It was silly, but she heard a wobble in her voice and had to blink away a tear.

"Don't be like that. The fitness is coming on, isn't it?"

Sally couldn't bring herself to deny it, but did tell Angela about her saddle sores. "The new clothes I bought were special padded cycling shorts and a windproof jacket. If they don't help it'll be back to the bus tomorrow."

"Well go and check they fit then. If not, you can exchange them before you go home."

"Thanks." Although convinced that the way her plans were going she'd get a puncture on the next journey, if not anything worse, Sally returned to the toilets. She'd just pulled on the distinctly unflattering shorts when Angela called her back to the phone.

"It's Señor Rodriguez again and he doesn't sound happy."

"When does he ever?" Sally muttered as she dashed out to take the call. Her part consisted of repeating, *perdone* and *lo siento* as well as *scusi*, which she feared wasn't even Spanish, whenever Señor Rodriguez paused for breath. She didn't manage to fit in many apologies.

As she was stammering away Alberto arrived. He stared at her outfit which, from the floor up, consisted of high heeled patent leather shoes, sheer stockings, padded cycling shorts, the thin anorak she'd hurriedly pulled on over her underwear so she could rush out into the office and a very flustered expression. That wasn't so good, but Alberto took over the phone call and somehow soothed Señor Rodriguez which was miraculous.

Alberto explained to both Sally and Angela that Señor Rodriguez had been calling to say he wasn't well and would have to postpone his trip to England. It was just after that Sally had launched into her 'good, very good' routine. Then of course she'd got him to call Wales when obviously Alberto was no longer there.

"No wonder he was annoyed," Sally said. "I'm really sorry, Angela. I've let you down and completely..."

Angela stopped her. "I see it was just a mistake, but it wouldn't have happened if you'd admitted you hadn't made much progress with your Spanish."

"Yeah, I know, but I felt such a failure. I might as well admit the cycling isn't going so well either. I have to change buses at Fareham and wait quarter of an hour there, but cycling still doubles my journey time."

"I didn't realise you travelled via Fareham, or that you were learning Spanish," Alberto said. "As I'm back here for a while, I could give you a lift and help with both problems at once."

Sally learned that, as well as living near to her, Alberto was a good language coach. Through April and May he picked her up and took her home every working day. Her Spanish, and their friendship, made considerable progress. When the weather got warmer Sally resumed her cycling, sometimes accompanied by Alberto. At first just short distances at the start or end of his longer rides, or down the pub for a drink.

Soon she was ready to try cycling to work again. Sally was delighted to discover she had sufficient breath to talk to Alberto on the way and sufficient vocabulary to do so in Spanish. Love was a*mar*, she learned, *guapa* meant beautiful and *matrimonio* was marriage.

By August, Alberto was again spending a lot of time in Wales and Sally spoke to Señor Rodriguez quite frequently. Fortunately he was as apologetic as she over the way their earlier attempts at conversation had gone. He explained he'd been in severe pain from kidney stones which made him grumpy and it had been difficult to concentrate which is why he'd not attempted to speak English. That was also why he'd put off flying to England, but now the stone was gone he'd be coming over. He was looking forward to seeing her in her shorts!

"Shorts?"

"That is the right word? Like small trousers for cycling in? I understand you were dressed in such an item when we had our unfortunate understanding."

When questioned, Alberto confessed that he'd described her appearance to help calm down the other man. "Sorry, but you did look funny."

The following March, Sally was again talking to Señor Rodriguez and very oddly dressed. She was half way through trying on the dress she'd bought for Alberto's wedding to Blodwynn, the girl he met and fell in love with during his visits to Wales. He'd invited all his colleagues to the service, as well as Señor Rodriguez who he'd met in person during the Spaniard's now regular visits to England.

Sally met Romeo Rodriguez on each occasion and they'd got on extremely well. In fact when he returned to Spain she was going with him. Just on holiday for now, but he'd hinted he'd like a more permanent arrangement. She'd at last sorted herself and got a love life. It was too soon yet to say if she'd live happily ever after, but Angela thought she would and as well as being 'smart' her friend was often right.

23. Sliding Into A Relationship

Holly tried to relax and concentrate on what Carl was whispering in her ear. It was no good; she tensed up whenever his child waved its sticky fingers around near her pastel coloured walls, gleaming white woodwork, crystal ornament, cream throws... It was clearly time for Carl and Jessica to go home and for Holly to consider where the relationship was going.

Once they'd left, Holly rushed around the house with wet wipes to remove every trace of their visit. No permanent damage had been done and finally she was able to relax.

She liked Carl a lot. If he'd been on his own she'd have asked him to move in. She liked the child too, at least as much as she liked any other child. Jessica was pretty and polite, but still a child.

Holly hadn't been alone long when the phone interrupted her thoughts. It was Mark, her best friend's husband.

"Anne has had to go into hospital again and this time she'll have to stay there until after the baby is born."

Holly's fingers tensed on the receiver. Poor Anne, the possibility of losing the baby must be torture to her – so must being away from her son, Joshua.

"Is there anything I can do?"

"Well, yes but... No, silly idea."

"What is it, Mark? I'll do anything. I know you're desperately worried..."

"Holly, it's OK. The doctor said Anne and the baby will be

fine if she rests. She'll probably need a Caesarian and it'll take a while for her to recover, but they'll make it."

"Of course. So what is it that would help but it'd be silly to ask me?"

"I can't pick Joshua up from school, not if I'm going to be taking time off work after Holly's Caesarian. We'll probably be able to get a childminder, but not for tomorrow."

"I see." It was simple really. A friend, with flexible working hours and house a short walk from Joshua's school, could easily collect him and take care of him until Mark finished work.

"What time does he finish?"

"Four tomorrow as he has football practice after school. I finish at five thirty, so could be at your place... I could collect him from whoever looked after him by six, maybe before."

Two hours with a child already worn out from football practice; she could do that for her best friend couldn't she?

"OK. I'll pick him up."

"You're a star, Holly. Anne will be so relieved; you know she wouldn't want him to be with a stranger. I'll let the school know."

The following day, Holly walked to the school.

"Aunty Holly!"

Joshua seemed pleased to see her and Holly attempted a convincing smile as she exchanged a few words with his teacher.

She was pleased that although there was mud on his boots, the rest of him looked clean. Asking him to remove the studded boots wasn't unreasonable and after he'd done that she could be confident he wouldn't mark her walls unless he ate anything. Would he need to eat before six? She hadn't thought to ask Mark.

"What do you normally do after school, Joshua?" she asked.

"Play with my friends or my train or make stuff with Lego or Play-doh or sometimes I do colouring or watch *Finding Nemo*."

Oh dear, she had nothing for him to do and no toys. He'd be so bored. No wonder little Jessica was sometimes fidgety or sulky when she visited. Holly remembered she'd not wanted the girl to play with her ball in case it knocked over a crystal ornament, hadn't allowed felt pens or paints in case she made a mess and hadn't wanted her to help make tea for the same reason. As a result, Jessica sat rigid on the sofa, clutching her doll. Holly realised she could have made more of an effort to provide suitable entertainment instead of thinking of the untidiness that might result.

"Can we go to the park please, Aunty Holly?" her young companion asked.

Although Joshua was dressed appropriately, Holly wasn't. Stupidly, she'd worn a short skirt and heels, so was too cold and uncomfortable to do anything other than rush straight home. Especially stupid as walking to the park and using the swings and roundabout would have filled most of the time before Mark was due to arrive. Next time, if there ever was a next time, she'd be better prepared. She could take Jessica to the park if there was a next time for her.

"Sorry, Josh. Aunty Holly isn't dressed for the park."

"Oh, OK. What are you dressed for?"

"Good question." Holly felt it was such a good question it deserved an honest answer. "I'm dressed so your teacher didn't think I was a crazy woman."

"Oh." He looked puzzled. "But Mummy said you are a crazy woman."

Holly couldn't help giggling as she imagined the look on Anne's face when she shared that gem. Anne claimed she was careful about what she said in front of Joshua as he repeated every ill-advised comment at precisely the moment it would cause most havoc.

Holly didn't doubt Anne really had called her crazy. They'd both been a little wild as children; motherhood for Anne and a responsible job for Holly had calmed them both down. Holly had calmed down more than Anne – perhaps Joshua kept her young and fun.

Fun? Holly wasn't fun any more. Instead of getting excited about colleagues' romances, Holly concentrated on spreadsheets. Instead of getting romantic with Carl, she worried about makeup on her clean linen. Instead of having a fun night out she sat in expensive wine bars wearing designer clothes... Holly couldn't decide when she'd stopped being fun but she knew when she was going to end it – right now!

She'd been a child herself once. All she had to do was remember what she'd liked doing then and allow Joshua to do the same. As he chatted about his school day she ran ideas through her mind. She'd liked being a bridesmaid for all her older cousins – getting dressed up in fancy dresses and having her picture taken and then later, skidding wildly across the dance-floor of the village hall. She liked making cakes with her mum and playing in the park with grandad and painting, and pretty much all the things she'd banned Jessica from doing.

Joshua wouldn't want to get done up in a dress, she didn't have paints or cake making ingredients but there must be something, she thought as she unlocked her door. She removed Josh's football boots and socks. He rushed ahead of her as she carried them to the safety of the recycling box and yesterday's newspaper. Once they were wrapped, she turned to watch Joshua almost doing the splits.

"You're floor is real slidy. I wish the football pitch was like this, then I'd have saved the goal."

"Oh? How?"

Josh demonstrated by running a few steps, then sticking one foot out in front and skidding into the dazzling white paint on her front door.

"Don't do that!" she shouted.

"Sorry, Aunty Holly. I forgot." He looked as though he might cry.

"Forgot what?"

"Daddy said not to run and not to touch anything in your house and just sit still and be good."

She guessed Carl had said the same to Jessica.

"It's OK, Josh, I'm not angry." She was, but only with herself. "If you go fast into the door you might hurt yourself." She was almost sure she'd been as worried about that as she had been about her paintwork. She knew which was the most important.

"We need something for you to land on."

"A pillow?" he suggested.

No, his aim might not be good. "Something bigger than that."

She took the quilt from the spare bed, removed its embroidered cover and arranged it to cover the door and skirting board.

"Try now."

Joshua managed a bit of a slide, but it didn't seem anything like as long as the skids she'd managed wearing her bridesmaid outfits. Maybe the lace-top socks she'd worn had helped.

"I think you'll have to put your socks back on."

Holly rubbed off as much mud as she could before he wriggled his feet back into them. The skid was better, but not fantastic. She thought back to her own technique.

"You need a run-up. Start in the kitchen."

Thank goodness she'd recently replaced the cream carpet with stylish ceramic tiles. The smears of football pitch shouldn't be too difficult to remove.

With a run-up, Josh skidded almost the entire length of the hallway. Not bad, but after arranging the quilt so carefully it seemed a shame for him not to whoosh right into it. Again she was thankful she'd recently taken up the carpet. She'd kept a decent sized off-cut in case it came in useful. At the time she'd been vaguely embarrassed about that – keeping things 'just in case' was the sort of thing her mother would do.

"Come on, Josh. You need a much bigger run-up."

"But you don't have any house left."

"No, but I've got a patio. Help me with the carpet and we'll make a runway."

They dragged the off-cut from the cupboard under the stairs and laid out the carpet and propped open the door.

"Go on, then."

"It's a long way," Joshua said.

Didn't Joshua want to take a small chance? Why should he; Holly never did. She couldn't risk getting close to Carl in case she got hurt. It wasn't just Jessica she was pushing away. Bravery was about more than risking physical injury. She was a bigger kid than Joshua. Used to be – as from half an hour ago she was both fun and brave. She walked out, barefoot, to stand by Josh. It did look a long way.

"I'll do it if you will," she said.

"I will if you go first," he countered.

"I'll have to borrow your socks." Holly's only footwear were sheer stockings that wouldn't survive the run-up.

They looked at each other's feet. There was no way Holly's would fit into Joshua's socks.

"Would you really do it if you had socks?"

"I really would."

Joshua took a deep breath, ran across the carpet-covered patio, through the kitchen and into the hall. He stuck a leg out in front, dropped onto one knee and skidded down the length of the hall. The sound of his thump into the quilt-padded front door was drowned by the wild cheering from the pair of them.

Joshua had a few more goes before deciding he was too tired and hungry to continue. Holly put the quilt back in the spare room, but didn't bother remaking the bed. It wouldn't matter if the spare room was untidy for one evening. She did put the carpet away though – she didn't want it to be spoilt as she might need it again soon.

"What do you normally eat after school?" she asked Joshua.

"Milk and biscuits."

Holly had milk, but the only biscuits were boring digestives she kept for when her mother visited. As a child she'd have wanted chocolate ones and guessed Joshua would feel the same way. She had chocolate – maybe they could make their own? Joshua was enthusiastic about that idea so Holly melted a bar of Green and Blacks in the microwave. They carefully spread the chocolate on the digestives. Well, as carefully as a five-year-old can manage. She couldn't persuade him to wait until they were set before sampling them, but that didn't seem to lessen his enjoyment. She did manage to extract a promise he'd sit still for a minute while she ran to the bathroom. To her relief he hadn't touched anything when she returned with her moisturising, make-up removing, wipes. They dealt with the melted chocolate, milk moustache and biscuit crumbs even more effectively than they coped with her waterproof mascara. His pink skin looked so smooth and fresh when she'd cleaned him up than she wondered if it were possible to buy a milk and cookies face-pack.

She was just considering what to do with Joshua next when her doorbell rang. It was Mark.

"I'm so sorry I'm late; the traffic..."

"No problem. We've had fun, haven't we, Joshua?"

"Yeah. Me and Aunty Holly have been doing power slides all frew the house and then cooking yummy biscuits."

"Right," Mark said doubtfully. "Of course you have."

"Aunty Holly is the bestest aunty in the whole world," Joshua declared.

Holly blinked a couple of times, glad her mascara was waterproof.

"I've got good news," Mark said. "Anne's mum can come and look after Joshua next week and we've got a childminder until then."

"Don't book the childminder. It'll cost you a fortune and

Anne won't like it. I can easily collect him for four more days."

Joshua cheered even louder than he'd done after the first slide, Holly wanted to join in and it looked as though Mark did to.

After waving them off, Holly went indoors and phoned Carl.

"I'd really like it if you and Jessica were to come round on Saturday."

"You're sure?"

"I'm sure."

"I'll bring a game for her to..."

"No don't do that; bring some socks. A pair for her and a pair for me."

It would need more than socks to put things right with Jessica, but another few days with Joshua would help equip her for the challenge.

24. Sailing Through Oxdjupet

The older couple had barely asked if they might share the table with Natalie and Dean, when an immaculate waiter appeared.

"A bottle of champagne, please," the man said.

Although Natalie and her partner's budget barely stretched to a glass of the house wine each with their evening meal, she didn't begrudge the others their extravagance. They were past retirement age and had probably worked hard to afford their luxuries.

It wasn't as though Natalie herself were on the bread-line. She and Dean had somewhere quite nice to live and, by booking early and choosing the cheapest cabin grade, could afford to take a cruise most years.

They'd been on enough now that the narrows along the Stockholm archipelago was their special place. Dean and Natalie both loved the way they seemed to sail through a carefree parallel universe. It was so peaceful that a child's laugh would easily reach them from the shore. They saw people boating and picnicking with their families making their own happy memories.

"I'm Donald, and this is my wife Gladys," the man said, bringing Natalie's attention back on board.

Gladys gave a finger-waggling wave, showing off a collection of expensive looking bracelets and rings.

Natalie didn't envy Gladys her jewellery either. She didn't have much herself other than her grandmother's brooch and the watch Dean had bought her ten years ago, but that was because she wasn't really a fan of jewellery. OK, there was one particular item she would like, but she certainly didn't need it.

Dean introduced himself, "And my partner Natalie."

"You're not married then?" Gladys asked.

Natalie's 'no' was sharper than she'd intended.

The waiter returned just then, to place champagne flutes on the table. He'd brought four.

"No..." Natalie started to explain he'd made a mistake.

"Please do join us in a glass," Donald said. "We're celebrating."

"It's our golden wedding anniversary," Gladys said.

Then Natalie really was jealous. Horribly, painfully jealous. The couple seemed lovely and they were being very generous. She was pleased to share in their happiness and who wouldn't like to unexpectedly be offered champagne, but...

Donald said, "Fifty years ago today! You two weren't even born then of course."

Natalie blinked back the tears she could feel welling up, plastered on a smile and asked how they had met.

"I was a typist and we met through work."

"Just like us," Dean said.

"Didn't take me long to realise she was the only woman for me," Donald said. "I proposed within a month, though it took a bit longer to talk her round."

So nothing like them at all, Natalie thought. It hadn't taken her long to decide Dean was the man for her. She'd dropped fruitless hints for weeks before giving in and asking him out. His acceptance had been instant and he'd immediately suggested somewhere to go, so she guessed he'd been working up to asking her himself.

When a few months later a work colleague had pointed out amazing deals on cruise prices it was Natalie who picked up a brochure. That sort of holiday really appealed to her and she was sure Dean would like it too. Eventually she suggested they go together.

Straight away he said, "How about this one? I've always been interested in Scandinavian history, particularly the Vikings. I'd would love to sail through the archipelago and see some of the places I've read about."

"Me too! Well not the Vikings, but I love the Stieg Larsson books and would like to see some of the places in them."

It was on that first cruise, just as they passed through the narrows that Natalie had told Dean she loved him. He didn't immediately say he loved her too; first he pulled her close and kissed her.

When they returned home, Natalie started to point out that they spent almost all their time together, either in her flat or his dark and slightly damp, terraced house.

"If we added my rent to the mortgage you already have, we could get somewhere rather nice," she said.

He'd nodded, but didn't suggest moving in together. It was Natalie who did that on their next cruise.

Straight away, Dean replied, "There are some nice looking places on the new estate they're building off the M27. It would be convenient for work and I'm sure we could afford one between us."

They'd not taken a cruise the following year; their free time and money had been used up decorating and furnishing the house. They'd managed it every year since though. All but one had taken them through the Stockholm archipelago; the only time they chose a completely different area they'd been very disappointed.

They'd gone to the Mediterranean which was too hot, especially for red haired Dean. The choppy return through the Bay of Biscay hadn't been any fun either. They'd not really needed to discuss sticking to the Baltic region in future.

Natalie hadn't dropped hints about getting married. There didn't seem any need when both their families and most of their friends were doing it. She had hoped that Dean would propose on their next cruise. He didn't, nor on the next. Family and friends seemed to give up on the idea, but Natalie didn't. What she wanted most in the world was for Dean to ask her to marry him. She continued to hope before their next cruise, but now after living with him for eight years, even she had begun to accept it just wasn't going to happen.

And it didn't matter, not really. Being married wouldn't make much difference to their lives, she knew. Just the one surname on their joint account chequebook, it'd be easier for people to know how to address Christmas cards, but nothing important.

A gold ring was no guarantee their relationship would last, they'd already lasted longer than most celebrity marriages, it seemed. It wasn't the wedding day she craved, though she was sure she'd love choosing a nice dress and sharing the service and reception with their friends and family. She didn't need to get married to have a big party though, in fact Dean had suggested holding one for her fortieth, but she'd said she'd rather put the money towards another cruise.

It was the proposal Natalie wanted. She wanted to know that Dean loved her enough to ask, not just to accept if she pushed him into it. He would accept if she asked, she was sure, but that wouldn't be the same at all.

She felt Dean touch her hand and glanced up to see three faces looking at her with a touch of concern.

There were full glasses of champagne on the table. She hadn't even heard the cork pop. Natalie gave herself a mental shake. She was not going to spoil Donald and Gladys's day, nor her and Dean's holiday by getting upset over something which really didn't matter.

"Sorry, I was miles away... well not that many actually, just down the archipelago at . It's where Dean first told me he loves me." It wasn't the kind of thing she'd normally share with strangers, but it seemed right to say it at that time, to this couple.

"Oh, how lovely!" Gladys said.

They all clinked glasses and drank to Donald and Gladys's fifty years and then to future happiness. Natalie sipped the sparkling liquid and willed her spirits to lift up to match the drink and the occasion. She almost succeeded.

Gladys waved to someone she recognised and beckoned them over. As friends of her and Donald joined them, Natalie and Dean thanked the couple, wished them well and slipped away.

"You OK?" Dean asked her once they were out of the restaurant.

"Of course."

He didn't look convinced. Of course he wasn't. He knew her far too well to be taken in. Why was she trying to hide her feelings anyway?

"I am OK, really. It's just that couple looked so happy, so secure."

"They did, didn't they? Oh! Is one of them ill or something?"

"Not as far as I know, but then how could I?"

"No, I suppose not. I just wondered why seeing them celebrate had upset you."

"I'm not upset exactly. It's just that it'll never be us, will it? We'll never be celebrating our fiftieth anniversary, will we?"

"Oh, Natalie, you're not ill, are you?"

"No." She saw the concern in his face, which told her more than any words, even the ones she longed to hear, could about his love for her. "I just meant the wedding anniversary part, because we're not married. We'll still be together in fifty years though, you don't get rid of me that easily!"

He'd kissed her then. "Glad to hear it."

"So, what are we going to do this afternoon? Do you fancy beating me at deck quoits again?"

"I could use my left arm?" Dean offered.

"Not a chance, mostly because you'd probably still beat me. You winning I can cope with, but not the humiliation of you doing it left handed."

"I wouldn't mention it often."

"No more than once an hour!" Natalie pretended to pout.

"You know me so well. Let's just enjoy sailing through the archipelago? We'll be at soon and we won't want to miss that."

"True. I'd better go and put some sunscreen on though if we're going to sit up top. It didn't look like it was going to be so sunny this morning, so I didn't bother."

"I did, but perhaps I should put on some more. Can you bring the bottle with you?"

"No problem."

"I'll meet you up where we sat the other evening then. Don't be too long."

"You're skin isn't as sensitive as all that!"

"No, but I'll miss you while you're gone."

She grinned. How could she doubt he really loved her? Natalie hurried down to their cabin, used the bathroom, changed into the strapless dress she knew Dean loved, slathered on lotion and climbed up to the top of the ship.

It was seven decks and she always used the stairs to help burn off the extra calories they consumed on holiday, but she didn't think she'd been gone long enough to account for the anxious look on Dean's face.

She went to kiss his cheek, but before she could he sort of sank in front of her. Was he suffering from sunstroke?

"Natalie," he took her hand. He was on one knee and holding a ring! "Will you marry me?"

"Yes! Oh yes, definitely!"

They hugged and kissed, then he pulled away for a moment to slip the slightly too big ring on her finger before kissing her again.

Gradually they became aware they'd attracted attention. Quite a crowd had gathered and were eager to congratulate them. Natalie asked one of the well-wishers to take their photograph.

"Sure thing. Do you want to get the ship's funnel in?"

"One like that, please but could you also take one of us

here?" Dean manoeuvred Natalie into position against the railing.

It wasn't until the phone was handed back and Natalie looked at the photo she realised he'd arranged it so was in the background; the exact spot where he'd proposed. That was appropriate for them. Perfect really.

News travelled quickly round the ship, so their conversation about whether they'd wait to tell their parents face to face, or try ringing them up with the good news was constantly interrupted.

"Let's wait until we're back," Natalie said. "They've waited long enough, another week or so won't matter and it'll be nice to see their reaction."

"Fine with me. Do you want to set a date for the wedding?"

"Worried I'll change my mind?"

"No, I'm not worried about that." His tone suggested there could be something else.

"You surely weren't worried I'd say no?"

"Not worried exactly, but I was a bit nervous. I suppose that's why it's taken me so long to get round to it."

She squeezed his hand.

"I know we've already had champagne today, but shall we order a bottle at dinner tonight?" Dean suggested.

"Let's. This is something to celebrate."

As Natalie returned to the cabin to get ready for dinner she had no idea why tears were once again building up, but she stepped into the shower and let them fall for a minute.

Who was she kidding? She knew exactly what was wrong. Dean hadn't asked her to marry him because it was what he wanted, but because after her reaction to Donald and

Gladys's anniversary and what she'd said about them not having one, he'd decided it was what she wanted. Natalie hadn't needed to go so far as proposing herself, but he'd only done it because he'd been pushed into it.

"Why doesn't he love me enough to actually want to marry me?" she sobbed to herself. She felt better afterwards and just a bit silly. Of course he wanted to. Dean never rushed into anything, the ten year wait was proof of that. Even if he'd felt he ought to ask, he wouldn't have rushed off to buy a ring and asked her immediately if he'd had any doubts.

He'd been nervous too she remembered. He wouldn't if he'd felt he was just going along with what she wanted, rather than wanting it himself would he?

She studied her face in the mirror. Good, there was no sign that she'd been crying. Wrapping a towel around her body she saw with horror there was something else there was no trace of; her ring! When had it come off? In the shower? Yes, there it was. Thank goodness for that.

Natalie rejoined her fiancé. "I think we'd better go back to the jewellers and get a chain to hang the ring on so I don't lose it."

"It is a bit big. They said if it didn't fit they'd change it, or could resize it."

"I'll have it resized. I want to keep this one. I'm impressed they can do that on the ship."

"The ship?"

"They'll have to, won't they? I don't want to wait until our next cruise to collect and wear it."

"Ah! No, I bought it from the jewellers in the High Street."

"At home? Before we left?"

"Actually, before we even booked this cruise. Months before. I kept losing the nerve to ask and then decided to do it at. It seemed the perfect place."

"It is; absolutely perfect." Her eyes filled with tears again, but this time she was crying from pure joy.

Thank you for reading this book. I hope you enjoyed it. If you did, I'd really appreciate it if you could leave a short review on Amazon and/or Goodreads.

To learn more about my writing life, hear about new releases and get a free short story, sign up to my newsletter – subscribepage.io/ItLSNa or you can find the link on my website patsycollins.co.uk

More books by Patsy Collins

Novels

Firestarter
Escape To The Country
A Year And A Day
Paint Me A Picture
Leave Nothing But Footprints
Acting Like A Killer

Little Mallow cosy mystery series

Disguised Murder and Community Spirit in Little Mallow
Dependable Friends and Deceitful Neighbours
in Little Mallow
Deadly Words and Innocent Gossip in Little Mallow

Non-fiction

From Story Idea To Reader
(co-written with Rosemary J. Kind)

A Year Of Ideas:
365 sets of writing prompts and exercises

All That Love Stuff

Short story collections

Over The Garden Fence
Up The Garden Path
Through The Garden Gate
In The Garden Air
Beyond The Garden Wall

No Family Secrets
Can't Choose Your Family
Keep It In The Family
Family Feeling
Happy Families

With Love And Kisses
Lots Of Love
Love Is The Answer

Slightly Spooky Stories I
Slightly Spooky Stories II
Slightly Spooky Stories III
Slightly Spooky Stories IV
Slightly Spooky Stories V

Just A Job
Perfect Timing
A Way With Words
Dressed To Impress
Coffee & Cake
Not A Drop To Drink
Criminal Intent
Crime In Mind
Making A Move